أنا مسلم

I am Muslim

P.A. DAVIES

First published as a paperback in 2020 by **MJD Publishing**, 920 Hyde Road, Manchester UK.
ISBN: 979-8-6325438-3-5
Copyright © Paul Anthony Davies 2018

COVER DESIGN: P.A.Davies
PROOF READERS: Caroline Vincent, Susan Keane & Susan McMillan

Though some of the events written within this book are based on fact, the overall **story and names** of the main characters portrayed are of a fictional nature and therefore not intended to represent any person or persons whether living or dead. Likewise, the views conveyed by certain characters throughout the novel are again, written within a fictional context and are not the views of the author or any other persons connected with this publication.

Please be aware that this book contains language and scenes of violence that some readers may find offensive and disturbing. It is, therefore, not suitable for persons under the age of eighteen or those who are easily offended or affected by such explicit adult themes. Neither the author nor the publishing company will be held responsible for any offence caused to any person who reads this novel notwithstanding the warning above.

A Personal Dedication

This book is dedicated to the families and friends of the twenty-two victims of the Manchester Arena attack, whose lives were tragically taken away on 22nd May 2017.

Saffie Roussos (8) Sorell Leczkowski (14) Eilidh MacLeod (14) Nell Jones (14) Olivia Campbell (15) Megan Hurley (15) Georgina Callender (18) Chloe Rutherford (17) Liam Curry (19) Courtney Boyle (19) Philip Tron (32) John Atkinson (26) Martyn Hett (29) Kelly Brewster (32) Angelika Klis (39) Marcin Klis (42) Elaine McIver (43) Michelle Kiss (45) Alison Howe (45) Lisa Lees (43) Wendy Fawell (50) Jane Tweddle (51)

Also dedicated to the people of Manchester who showed great strength, resolve and solitude at a time when the city needed it most.

My thoughts and my prayers go out to you all.

P.A.Davies

ALSO WRITTEN BY P.A.DAVIES

LETTERBOX
ISBN: 978-0-09572639-0-1
A fictional story based around the IRA bombing of Manchester in June 1996.

GEORGE: A GENTLEMAN OF THE ROAD
ISBN: 978-0-09572639-1-8
A true tale of one of Manchester's homeless fraternity. Funny, sad and heart-warmingly bizarre. This is George's story.

THE GOOD IN MISTER PHILIPS
ISBN: 978-0-9572639-3-2
An erotic thriller, where nothing is what it seems.

NOBODY HEARD ME CRY
ISBN: 978-0-9572639-7-0
A gritty, true-life story set in the darker side of Manchester. A world of drugs, prostitutes and gangs. A world where nobody hears you cry.

ABSOLUTION
ISBN: 978-0-9572639-8-7
1992: A civil war rages in South Sudan. Jada - a sixteen-year old boy - sets out on a treacherous journey to rescue his younger sister who is kidnapped by Militia for trafficking to the highest bidder.

"In a world full of imagination
anything is possible!"

"Whoso kills a soul, it shall be as if he had killed all mankind; and he who saves a life, it shall be as if he had given life to all mankind." ... **Quran 5:53**

"Do not let the hatred of a people prevent you from being just. Be just; that is nearer to righteousness." ... **Quran 5:8**

One

Compared to what the weather had been like previously, the day was unusually warm and sunny especially given that it was only 9am. That said, Kyle didn't give a second thought to the current spate of high pressure, other than to be subconsciously grateful that the steps he was now sitting on were dry.

He held his head in his hands and closed his eyes, dwelling on what had been and what was yet to come. The last few weeks had been like an agonising nightmare but - unlike nightmares encountered whilst sleeping - this was one he could never wake up from. Maybe, in the unforeseeable future, things would get better but Kyle couldn't see it happening. Not soon, not ever. He was trapped inside it all and it hurt like fuck.

"Cheer up mate, it might never happen!" A chirpy, unfamiliar voice said, immediately snapping Kyle out from his troubled thoughts.

He looked up and stared at two men now standing in front of him.

"Too late mate," he replied solemnly. "It already has."

***

Two

The telephone rang for quite some time before the fifty-five year old man pressed the mute button on the TV's remote and wearily picked up the mobile phone from the arm of his chair.

"Hello." He said, after thumbing the green connect button.

"Kasim. Turn on your television?" Came an anxious response.

"I'm already watching it Hazan. Such terrible news!"

"Yes, I know. Wasn't Ecrin supposed to be going there tonight? Does she know yet?"

Kasim shuddered. He had already considered the *what-ifs* many, many times during the past ten minutes and now, sitting here - with a phone in his hand and his eyes glued to the silent television broadcast - he found himself dwelling on those same *what-ifs* once again.

"Kasim?" Hazan asked softly "Are you still there?"

Kasim exhaled a long breath and wiped away the formation of a tear with the heel of his free palm. "Yes, sorry Hazan, I'm still here. Ecrin is asleep so she hasn't heard yet."

On the other end of the telephone, Hazan frowned, as silence prevailed once more. "What is it Kasim?" He quizzed. "Are you okay?"

"Am I wrong to thank Allah, with all my heart, that Ecrin was too poorly to go to the concert, Hazan?" He finally asked. "Or does this make me a bad man?'

"No, no, no Kasim, you are not to think like that," Hazan responded, firmly. "If anything, it only shows that you are a good and loving father. What has happened tonight is very, very tragic but we must thank Allah for each and every mercy that he shows. He, nor anybody else, will condemn you for giving thanks that your daughter is safe!"

"But they are saying that ... that children have been badly injured, maybe even killed and ..."

"And Allah will punish those responsible Kasim," Hazan cut in.

"And what about the Manchester community Hazan? Who will they punish?"

"I'm not sure I ..."

"The news reporters have already suggested that this was the work of some Muslim extremist from ISIS," Kasim quickly continued. "So who do you think that retribution will be sought against?"

"But we are *Turkish* Muslims Kasim, not Iraqis or Syrians. Surely they will see..."

"The ignorant only see a label hanging from the colour of a man's skin Hazan, not the man beneath it. You know this. Don't you remember what happened after nine-eleven?"

"What? The broken windows at the restaurant you mean? We don't know that that was anything to do with what happened in America Kasim, we agreed on that!"

"No," Kasim retorted sharply. "You dismissed it as coincidence but not me. I don't believe in coincidence!"

3

"So what are you saying?" Hazan asked. "That we should go into hiding like frightened rats?"

"No. I'm just saying that we should be very careful over the next few weeks, months even. The residents of Manchester will mourn this day and rightly so, but a few will use this tragedy as an excuse to display their inherent hate for Muslims. Turkish we may be Hazan, but whichever way you want to look at it, we are still Muslims living in Manchester."

*

Outside the open living room door, Kasim's seventeen-year-old son, Mehmet, sat on the staircase listening to his father. Like his father, he too was thankful that his fourteen-year-old sister was upstairs and in bed – safe, alive – but he was also harbouring his own concerns.

Thirty minutes earlier, a suspected bomb had been detonated in a concert hall no more than three miles from where he lived: a concert hall where his best friend's sister - Abby – and mother had gone that evening. Just two excited fans that would have been a trio, had Mehmet's sister been well enough to go with them.

Mehmet took a phone from his pocket, looked at the screen and frowned. Still no reply to the messages he had sent to his friend. He brought up the call log, touched the name *Kyle* on the screen for the umpteenth time that evening and held the phone to his ear whilst the call connected.

"This is Kyle and clearly I ain't here. Leave a message or whatever an' I'll call you back ... maybe?"

Mehmet sighed and waited for the beep.

"Kye, it's me again man. Hope everything is okay with … y'know, your sister and stuff? Call me back mate, yeah?"

Mehmet disconnected the call, placed the phone back into his pocket and put his head in his hands.

"Any luck yet Mehmet?" The unexpected sound of his father's voice at the foot of the stairs caused Mehmet to jump. "Sorry son. I just wondered if...?"

"No, nothing yet Pop. I've sent texts and left voice messages but …" Mehmet shrugged.

"They'll be fine son, I'm sure of it!" Kasim offered, trying to reassure his son, although he himself wasn't convinced by the attempt.

"I don't know Pop," Mehmet doubted. "It just doesn't feel right, you know?"

Kasim nodded. "Let's see what happens son. There is no point in second guessing things." He began to climb the stairs, putting a hand onto his son's shoulder as he passed, "I'm going to check on your sister. Try not to worry Mehmet. Allah will do what is right. Of that I *am* sure!"

Just over four weeks later, Kasim Yilmaz - a man who lived by the teachings and guidance of the Quran - would not only come to question that particular surety but also, the actual existence of Allah himself.

***

Three

In the winter of 1968, the family Yilmaz upped sticks, left their home in the Sultanahmet District of Istanbul, Turkey and immigrated to England. Not because of the two years constant badgering to do so by Baba Yilmaz's brother, Omer - already a resident and small restaurant owner in Manchester – but because Baba Yilmaz feared for the safety of his wife and his children. Economic recession and social unrest plagued Turkey and Baba Yilmaz knew that years of repression, martial law and distaste for the government of the time, would almost certainly lead to an uprising of some description. He wasn't wrong, as 1970 saw another military coup in Turkey and a new, more intense wave of violence courtesy of the Turkish People's Liberation Army. The Yilmaz family may not have had much in 1970s England but at least they had their health and their freedom.

Kasim Yilmaz was just six-years-old when he and his family came to England, the initial announcement of which made him both confused and sad. Confused, because he couldn't understand why he had to leave his friends behind and sad because his dog, Micha, had to live with the neighbour forever more.

"But Orhan bey doesn't even like Micha," Kasim pleaded. "He throws stones at him!" The lie-tainted plea was of course in vain. Micha took up resident in Mr Orhan's home and Kasim believed that his once happy life would never see the light of happiness, ever again. However, on the very first day that he stepped foot onto British soil, all that confusion and sadness he had felt in his homeland, dissipated faster than the snow melting under his shoes; an element of winter that he had never seen before. He felt excited and a little scared by what this new country had to offer but above all else, he felt … well … he felt bloody freezing.

In the inner cities of England during the '60s and early '70s, it was not unusual for the young children of an immigrant family to be home-schooled, although that concept usually consisted of working long hours in whatever business their parents had established. Unlike his brother - whose only son had worked in the family restaurant from just nine-years old - Baba Yilmaz wasn't of that mind-set and insisted that his sons attend school and attain the skills and qualifications needed to survive in such a competitive world.

"But I want to do what you do Baba," Kasim said. "With cousin Hazan!"

"And wait on tables all your life? What kind of future is that?" Baba Yilmaz replied.

"But I…"

"There are no *buts* Kasim. Get yourself an education, learn the English language and one day you might own a chain of restaurants for yourself."

Kasim mulled over the words of his father and - despite it being a foregone decision anyway -agreed to attend school, work hard and make his father proud.

"Good boy," Baba Yilmaz said, hugging his youngest son.

*

So it was that Kasim studied hard and tried to make his father proud, which he regularly did. According to his teachers, Kasim was bright and well mannered and actually wanted to learn all that he could: an unusual trait for a now thirteen-year old boy in a state comprehensive school of inner city Manchester.

"A credit to Moss Street High." Was the usual accolade of his educational peers.

At sixteen however, Kasim's personal life was thrown in to turmoil when his father and uncle Omer were killed in a car accident whilst travelling from Manchester to Sheffield via a snow-laden road known as the *Snake Pass*. This tragedy clearly impacted on Kasim's education too, because he left school that same year without a single qualification to his name. His teachers were highly surprised and his mother equally disappointed, but there was nobody more upset with the results than Kasim himself; years of study, years of making his father proud, eliminated in a whisper.

Asides from the grief and educational disaster, the untimely deaths of his father and uncle brought about another burden for the troubled teenager to bear. With neither of his two elder brothers being able to take over the reins, it was down to Kasim to step in and help his cousin Hazan with the restaurant. After all, with very little savings and no life insurance, the family would have virtually nothing to live on if the restaurant ever closed down. A sixteen-year-old child and his uneducated, nineteen-year-old cousin, entrusted to keep the family business afloat? Not a combination that would encourage a vote of confidence for survival. But - with some guidance and advice from his mother - Kasim didn't just *help*

Hazan with the restaurant, he completely ran it. In fact, he ran it so well that in the spring of 1986 the family managed to open a second, much larger venue in the centre of Manchester. Brits - it seemed - had a love of Turkish food, especially after a night of clubbing and drinking.

In that same year, Kasim interviewed an eighteen-year-old Turkish girl called Azra Tekin for the position of waitress at the new restaurant. When he told her that she hadn't got the job, she wanted to know why.

"Because." Kasim began, with a confidence that was bordering on arrogance. "No future wife of mine is becoming a waitress!" He didn't care how it sounded, he was smitten with the girl the moment she had walked through the door.

The girl held his stare for a while and gave him a wry smile. "And no future husband of mine," she said. "Will ever tell me what I can or cannot do with my life!" She stood up and held out her hand. "Thank you for wasting my day Yilmaz bey!" She offered, sarcastically.

Kasim stood up, took her hand into his own and smiled. "And thank you for making mine, Tekin hanim," he replied. As she released his grip and began to walk away, Kasim decided to throw caution to the wind. "Oh, one more thing before you go, Tekin hanim?" The girl turned around, raised an inquisitive eyebrow but said nothing. "Erm, seeing as you're not going to be an employee of mine," Kasim continued, suddenly feeling a lot less confident. "I was sort of hoping that I could take you out sometime?"

The girl looked at Kasim, gave an encouraging smile and stepped towards him. "In that case," she replied, softly. "It looks as though we are both going to be disappointed today, doesn't it?" She watched his expression change and his shoulders droop before turning once again to walk out of the office.

Within two hours, Kasim was on the phone offering Miss Tekin a position in his restaurant. Just over three months later, she finally agreed to go out with him. One year on - in the summer of 1987 - Mr Kasim Yilmaz and Miss Azra Tekin were joined together in holy matrimony.

On 25th July 2017, Mr and Mrs Yilmaz were due to celebrate their 30th wedding anniversary with a host of family and friends. However, a tragic sequence of events beforehand, were set to overshadow that particular celebration and darken many more to follow.

****

Four

On the day that the boy came into this world, his father held the tiny bundle close to his chest and wept. His wife Azra watched on, smiling yet silent. She knew exactly what her husband had seen in the child because she had seen it too the moment the midwife had placed the newborn into her arms.

"He looks like Baba," Kasim whispered, not taking his eyes off his third son.

"I know, my love." Azra replied. "And I was thinking. Maybe we should let him take Baba's name?"

Kasim turned to his wife and nodded. "Baba would have liked that," he said with a sodden smile. "Thank you." He looked back down at his son - gazing up at him through bright, brown eyes - and gently stroked his head. "As long as I have a breath inside me," he whispered. "I will love and protect you with all my life. Welcome to the family, Mehmet Yilmaz."

Two years later - in the autumn of 2002 - Kasim Yilmaz was on the move for the second time in his life, taking his family from their home in Fallowfield, South Manchester, to Cheetham Hill in the north. Kasim announced that the move was due to the cramped conditions of their existing home but in truth, it was much more sinister than that.

*

11

In 2001, the Yilmaz family was one of only three Muslim families living on a road in Fallowfield otherwise dominated by white British and black Jamaican residents. They were also the only Turkish family in the area, with the other two Muslim families having originated from Pakistan. All the neighbours knew that the Yilmaz's were Turkish and some of them had actually visited the family restaurant. Kasim recalled the odd phrase, *mate's rates*, being explained to him by his white neighbour Terry and subsequently giving Terry and his friends a regular discount. Kasim didn't mind as Terry had always invited Kasim and his family into his home for summer barbeques and New Year's Eve parties. It was a nice community to be a part of and - given the cultural diversity - relatively close-knit. However, post 11th September 2001 that situation changed dramatically.

*

It started subtly of course - the occasional strange look, neighbours seemingly avoiding conversation - but then the momentum grew. No more invites or visits from Terry, eggs thrown at the house, a window smashed at the restaurant, stones thrown at the house, paint thrown at the house, and human faeces left on the doorstep. The anonymous note pushed through the letterbox was the final straw.

"Any idea why you are being targeted?" The young Police Officer had asked, once Kasim had finally reported the incidents, almost six months later. "Have you fallen out with anybody?"

"Officer. I know exactly why we have become targets!" Kasim replied, angrily. "The same reason that the Patels at number seventy-one and the Khans at eighty-five have become targets too!" The officer raised an eyebrow. "It is because we are Muslims." Kasim continued. "And therefore, by definition in the dictionary of the stupid, we are fully responsible for the atrocities that occurred in America!"

The Police Officer frowned. "You think that you are being harassed because of what happened to the Twin Towers last year?"

"I don't think it officer." Kasim replied, pulling a piece of paper from his pocket. "I know it."

PC Richards took the paper from Kasim and unfolded it, sighing with disgust when he saw what was on it. There was a crude, almost child-like drawing on the paper that showed a house. On the front door of the house was the number of the Yilmaz residence with the blazing tail end of a plane jutting out from the roof. Underneath the picture the words *How would you like it you cunts* - together with - *watch this space,* had been added in bright red. It was as pathetic as it was unnerving.

Every official body knew that to do little about this particular complaint would be foolhardy especially if things went tits-up in the future. Thus, with the risk of huge explanations and mountains of paperwork being greater than the perceived threat, the Housing Authorities - on the recommendation of the Police - arranged for the Yilmaz family to be moved to what they believed was a safer, more Muslim-friendly area of Manchester. Why investigate the problem when you can remove the cause? As pathetic a policy as it was publically unofficial.

Nevertheless, the anti-social behaviour towards the Yilmaz family stopped. The Police were seen to

13

have taken positive action and the housing authorities had a reliable, rent-paying family living in one of their less desirable residence. Everyone's a winner … for the foreseeable at least.

***

Five

Mehmet Yilmaz and Kyle Roberts had been friends for as long as they could remember. They had attended the same pre-school together, the same primary school and the same high school, although Kyle would be the first to admit that Mehmet was the brighter of the two. Kyle, on the other hand, was the stockier and the one who wasn't afraid to stick up for himself.

The area in which Mehmet grew up was culturally diverse – White British, Pakistani, Indian, West African, Irish, Polish, Jamaican, Chinese and of course, Turkish - with each sub-culture minding their own business and each tolerating the religions and practices of the other. Most people in the local community knew Mehmet as a polite, smart and accommodating young man who didn't have a bad bone in his body.

In contrast, Kyle grew up in an area no more than three miles from Mehmet's home yet the cultural diversity there almost mirrored the Yilmaz's former hometown of Fallowfield. White British families dominated the area with much more than a handful of them firmly against change. For them, alternative religions – that is, those that were not ordained by the sacred churches of Manchester City or Manchester United - were begrudgingly tolerated. But … *"Don't ever come to my gaff trying to convert me mate!"*

Kyle Roberts was known by his local community as, the boy that came from *that* family: a family that was no stranger to the likes of Social Services or the Police. Kyle's eldest brother, Thomas, was currently serving a three-year sentence at HMP Strangeways for an aggravated domestic burglary, whilst his younger brother, Michael, was the one with ADHD; the sibling who was constantly smashing up his room or threatening his parents with causing harm to them or to himself. Social Services, teachers, specialist behavioural units and doctors did what they could for Michael - which in essence, was only the bare minimum of duty bound care - with all of them predicting that in time, Michael would undoubtedly join his brother Thomas on the criminal career path. When this *non-official* deduction was first reached, Michael Roberts was just eight-years old.

Other than a couple of Police warnings (Mrs Roberts) and one fine for public order offences (Mr Roberts) - together with a string of domestic related incidents between the two - Mum and Dad were relatively crime free. They hated politics, they hated the Police, they hated the council and they hated England becoming a free for all.

"Don't mind who comes 'ere." Mr Roberts had often announced. "As long as they contribute and pay their way like we all 'ave to!"

Fine words indeed, from a man who - unlike his wife - hadn't worked for many years. Not legitimately anyway. Well, he couldn't afford to lose his disability allowance and other government benefits by working now, could he?

Despite being labelled as the product of a dysfunctional family, Kyle actually liked and took an interest in school. He was never going to be the country's top academic but if there were ever an award for consistently good effort, he would be up there on the centre podium. But he didn't just attend school for himself, he also did it for his sister Abby, three years his junior. He needed - wanted - to set an example for her that his brother Thomas had failed to do for him and, likewise, his parents for Thomas. He had seen how some of the local girls of his age group - and younger - strived for nothing more than being some wannabe gangster's moll. Their misguided idea of education was getting wasted on cheap alcohol whilst being only too willing to give out hand-jobs to the local *scrotes* in return for a bit of weed. This, Kyle vowed, was not the path his sister would take and, as such, became overly protective of her. There were a few disgruntled words from Abby about this particular arrangement once she'd entered her teen years, but in the main, she followed Kyle's guidance. The result? Her schoolwork was excellent and her friends decent. Ironically, her best friend was Mehmet's sister Ecrin, with whom she shared the same taste in music and teen idols, and the same distaste for the company of boys. That would undoubtedly change the older she became but for now, Kyle could relax. A little.

*

Kyle's father - Alan Bryan Roberts - had an indoctrinated attitude of indifference towards non-white people. He wasn't racist per se, just badly educated and influenced by an era that found the cultural labels of *Coloureds, Pakis* and *Chinks* socially acceptable. He revelled in distasteful humour about race and sex, enjoyed lager - canned not bottled - and harboured a strong opinion on every religion, every political party and every football match ever played by Man City and England. Alan's idea of change was watching Mrs Roberts apply a new colour scheme to the walls of their lounge each year; a routine he didn't subscribe to but always had an opinion on. He believed that an Englishman's home was his castle and that homes in England should remain solely the castles of Englishmen.

To a decent society, Alan was a bigoted, self-centred man who constantly hung the flag of St George outside his bedroom window: not as an act of patriotism but as an act of defiance against the politically correct housing association that banned its *permanent* display outside their properties.

For those like-minded people in Alan's world, he was the salt of the earth, a rough diamond with a heart made of solid gold. Never too shy to put a hand in his pocket and buy a round, never too busy to listen and advise … unless the football was showing on his forty-eight inch plasma TV of course.

In contrast to Mrs Roberts, Alan's love for his children was felt - and displayed - in varying degrees, usually dependant on his moods, but always dependant on which child he was talking to or about at the time. He felt disappointed in his eldest son though maintained that Tommy was actually a good lad who had fallen in with the wrong crowd. One could argue - as a prosecution barrister had - that Tommy hadn't been in a crowd when he burgled Edna Jones' home and threatened the frail seventy-eight-year old with a kitchen knife. Unlike his father, the jury failed to see any goodness in Thomas Roberts during his trial and subsequently found him guilty. The Judge - who had already formed his opinion of the accused prior to the verdict being reached - vehemently gave the smirking little shit before him, the sentence he deserved.

"In my opinion Roberts," Mr Harris QC had voiced about the prison term imposed. "Three years is not long enough. But unfortunately, I am bound by the sentencing rules of our current legal system." He sighed and shook his head in dismay, knowing that the defendant would no doubt forget what the elderly Mrs Jones would never be able to. "Take him down please officer!"

Of his second son, Kyle, Alan wondered why the boy was putting so much effort into his schoolwork and why he was actually looking forward to college.

"The Benefits Office doesn't need you to have GCSEs to sign-on you know?" Alan had said, with his usual embrace of negativity. "And believe you me sunshine, given the state of the country, that's the only place you'll be heading in the long run!"

Had it been a decade earlier, Alan would have insisted that his son leave school at sixteen and start contributing financially to the household. However, given that the Government had changed the law to keep children in education until they reached the age of eighteen, the Roberts family would continue to receive child benefit for Kyle. Not all bad then.

Other than his Kyle's obsession with wanting to be a swot, there was something else that niggled Alan about his son; in particular, the company he kept. Alan wasn't saying that Mehmet was a bad person, not at all. It was just that … well … he was different. Why Kyle couldn't hang around with lads of his own kind was beyond all comprehension to Alan. *And* - if that wasn't enough - his daughter Abby had adopted the same bizarre mentality as Kyle and was seemingly closer to Mehmet's sister than she was her own younger brother.

"Oh Alan," his wife had sighed. "Don't be so ridiculous. She's just a young teenager, and everything's about BFFs and pop music at that age."

"BB what?" Alan frowned.

Angela raised her eyes and shook her head. "BFF, not BB," she replied with a titter. "It stands for *best friends forever*. What century are you living in love?"

"One where brothers and sisters are close and love each other, no matter what!"

"She *does* love Michael," Angela insisted. "He's her brother."

"Then she should show it a bit more," Alan replied. "Instead of constantly picking on him like she does. No wonder he's an angry little sod!"

"You can't blame Abby for our Michael's condition Alan, that's not fair. You know what he's like!"

"Well. She doesn't help matters does she?" Alan retorted. "I've heard her making fun of him, especially when she's showing off to that Paki girl!"

"Shush!" Angela warned sternly, raising a finger towards her lips. "Ecrin's up in Abby's room and she'll hear you!"

"I don't really give a fuck!" Alan shrugged.

"No, but your daughter does!"

"Hmm."

"And for the millionth time, Mister Uneducated, Ecrin's of Turkish descent, not Pakistani."

"Whatever," Alan replied, waving a dismissive hand. "Still a Muslim though, isn't she? I'm surprised that her uncles or whatever, haven't started grooming Abby yet!"

"Now that's enough!" Angela snapped. "I won't have that disgusting talk in this house Alan. What the fuck has gotten into you?"

Alan shot up from his chair and hastily folded up the newspaper he had been trying to read. "Fuck this," he hissed, almost to himself. "I'm going for a dump!"

"Good," Angela said, sarcastically. "Let's hope you get rid of *all* your crap whilst you're up there!"

"Maybe I will, maybe I won't," Alan snorted, walking away. "But I bet you're still 'ere when I come down?"

"Don't bank on it arsehole," Angela replied bitterly, as Alan disappeared into the hallway. "And make sure you open the window when you've done?" She shouted out. "Me Mum and Dad are coming later and I don't want them gassing!"

"Really?" Alan said to himself. "I couldn't think of anything better!"

As he reached the top of the stairs, Alan heard music blaring from his daughter's room, the boom-boom-boom adding to his already developing headache.

"Abby!" He called out. "Turn that rubbish down will you?"

Seconds later, the music was lowered and Abby's bedroom door flew open.

"It isn't rubbish dad," Abby called out towards the closing bathroom door. "And it's way better than that old-fashioned, pensioner stuff you listen to!"

"Yeah, whatever Abby," Alan called back. "Just keep it down!"

Abby scowled and immediately did something that she would never - ever - do in front of her dad. She flicked two fingers up, before going back into her bedroom and slamming the door on her personal space.

"He's such an idiot," she moaned, sitting on the bed, next to her best friend.

"That's dads for you," Ecrin said, raising her eyebrows. Ironically, Ecrin didn't think the same about her own father though, not in the slightest.

*

5th March 2017

"Happy birthday dear Abby ... Happy birthday to you!"

The Roberts family (bar Thomas of course) cheered loudly as the birthday girl blew out the fourteen candles on her cake.

Abby loved the perfume from Kyle, appreciated the shopping voucher off Michael (even though he didn't have a clue that he'd bought it ... so, thanks mum) and nearly passed out when she opened the present from her parents. In fact, she cried.

"Oh my god, oh my god! How? When? I, I thought they were all sold out?"

"We got them the first day they went on sale," Mum ginned widely. "And look," she added, pointing to the concert tickets. "We're right near the front!"

"Oh wow!" Abby giggled. "That's so cool!" She gave her parents a hug and a kiss, the likes of which her dad hadn't gotten since her last birthday.

"And there's something else," Mrs Roberts announced, her eyes now welling slightly at her daughter's joy. Abby frowned. "We figured that you wouldn't want to go with just your mum, so …" She reached into a drawer behind her and produced a third ticket. Abby gasped. "This one's for whichever one of your friends is worthy enough to come with us."

With a mixture of a high-pitched scream, happy tears and laughter, the fourteen-year-old girl embraced her parents once again. "This is the best birthday ever," she sobbed. "Thank you so much!"

"I wonder who she'll invite to the concert?" Kyle asked knowingly, winking at his mum.

"Erm, Ecrin, obviously," Abby replied, turning quickly towards her favourite brother. "She loves Ariana as much as I do."

"Oh, I'd never have guessed that one." Kyle stuck his tongue out at Abby before giving her a hug. He'd never seen his sister so giddy and excited as she was today, but then again, she'd never gotten a ticket to see her favourite pop star before. If she was this hyper now, he mused, what would she be like on the actual day of the concert?

Tragically, somebody already had an answer to that particular question.

***

23

Six

"Oh wow Ecrin, thank you!"

"It's not much, but …"

"Are you jokin'? I love it." Abby beamed. "Hug," she added, holding out her arms towards her friend.

"I'm glad you like it." Ecrin said, embracing the birthday girl.

When they parted, Abby admired her gift again and then held it out. "Will you?" She asked.

"Course I will." Ecrin replied, taking the bracelet and fastening it around Abby's wrist.

The bracelet - purchased from *Claire's Accessories* the previous weekend - was made up of six small, silver, metal blocks through which was threaded, a strip of rounded, black leather. On the four centre blocks, the letters *A B B Y* had been stamped with baby pink enamel whilst the two end blocks displayed a bright red heart on each. The value? Just four pounds ninety-nine pence but to Abby, it was priceless.

Once Ecrin had fastened the bracelet, Abby held out her wrist in front of her, admiring her present.

"So," Ecrin continued. "What else did you get?" Abby lowered her arm and grinned. She leant towards her bedside cabinet, opened the top drawer and withdrew an envelope, as her friend looked curiously on. "OMG!" Ecrin screamed when she saw the concert ticket. "You're going to see Ariana. That's sic. Oh wow, you're so lucky!"

"That's not all," Abby said, leaning back over to the drawer. When she produced another ticket for their favourite pop star's gig - and told Ecrin it was for her - Ecrin gasped, cried, hugged Abbey and cried some more. "Will your dad let you come?" Abby asked, only too aware of how protective her father was.

"I don't care what he says," Ecrin replied. "I'm not missing this, even if it means lying to him!"

Though both girls laughed they both knew that Ecrin would never lie to her dad and actually did care what he said. They also knew that it would be down to Ecrin's brother Mehmet to convince Mr Yilmaz that everything would be okay and get his approval. What Ecrin would do without her brother, she just didn't know.

*

Monday 22nd May 2017

Abby disconnected the call on her mobile phone and sighed.

"I take it she's not coming then?" her mum asked.

Abby glanced towards her dad - who was reading the local newspaper - and then up towards her mum, standing by a humming microwave oven currently zapping some tomato soup.

"Why doesn't that surprise me?" Alan mumbled.

"Oh be quite Alan," Angela retorted. "The girl can't help being poorly!"

Alan lowered his newspaper and frowned. "Poorly, my arse," he returned. "It'll be against her religion or something. Trust me, being *poorly* is just a lame excuse!"

"Dad!" Abby scolded. "It has nothing to do with her religion, she's got flu … or do Muslims not get that in your world?"

"Don't be a smart arse Abby," Alan shot back, crossly. "You're not too old for a crack you know?"

"Okay, whatever dad," Abby groaned, as she stood up and quickly left the room. She didn't want him to see her crying.

"Why do you have to be so insensitive with your daughter, for God's sake?" Angela snapped, once she'd heard Abby climbing the stairs. "She's a fourteen-year old girl who happens to be very upset. You could've at least been nice for once in your miserable life!"

Alan folded the newspaper and laid it down on the table. "It's not my bloody fault she's feeling hormonal and, for the record, it's not my fault that her so-called friend has let her down, either!" He removed a mobile phone from his pocket, brought up his contact list of fifteen people and pressed the third in line.

"Who you calling?" Angela quizzed.

"Billy," Alan replied.

"Billy? Billy who?"

"How many Billys do we know?" Alan countered.

"Why you calling…" Angela stopped short when Alan suddenly held up his hand and began speaking into his phone.

"William my good man. It's Alan."
Pause.

"Yeah, good mate thanks. You?"
Pause.

"Nice one, nice one. Listen Bill, how you fixed for buying a ticket for this concert at the Arena tonight?"

Angela looked on and shook her head with utter disbelief. *He would sell his own mother's clothes whilst she was still warm in her coffin, he would!* She thought, bitterly.

"Fuck me Billy," Alan continued, regardless of the icy stare from his wife. "You serve time for robbery you know?"

Pause.

"Yeah, yeah, I know you have to re-sell it but Jesus. It's almost a front row seat man. You'll have no trouble shifting it to some starry-eyed teenager!"

Pause.

"Yes William. Now that's more like it. Right, I'll drop it off at yours in a bit, yeah?"

Pause.

"Oh? Which one?"

Pause.

"Okay mate, nice one. I'll see you in the *Fletcher's* later then. The first round is on you though, ha-ha!"

Pause!

"Yeah, yeah. Sweet. Okay Bill, I'll catch you in a bit. Ta-rah pal … Yeah, will do. Ta-rah mate, ta-rah!"

Alan placed the mobile phone back into his pocket and looked up towards his scowling wife. "What?" He asked, shrugging his shoulders. "No point in it going to waste is there? And I doubt that Ecrin's family will be stumping up the cost of a wasted ticket!"

"How much?"

"What?"

"You heard me Alan Roberts. How much is Billy giving you?"

"Erm, fifty quid."

"Fifty?" Angela repeated, angrily. "It cost a lot more than that Alan!"

"Hey, he offered me thirty to start with," Alan replied. "So, given that the concert starts in a few hours, I think fifty notes is a pretty good price."

"It would have been nice to have been consulted with first though, before *you* decided to sell it!"

"Well," Alan said, removing his mobile phone once more. "I can always call him back and cancel ... if you want it sitting in your bag as an expensive memento that is?"

"Such a dick!" Angela exclaimed, as Alan chuckled. "I want to see all of that fifty pounds as well," she added, sternly. "I don't want to hear that you've blown it in the pub or lost it on some stupid bet!"

"Worry not my precious," Alan assured her as he stood up from the table. "The money will be in your purse before you leave tonight, trust me?"

"Trust you?" Angela laughed. "I wouldn't trust you as far as I could throw you!"

"Ooo," Alan gasped, holding a hand against his heart. "You cut me deep woman."

"Piss off," Angela responded, throwing a tea towel at her husband.

Alan caught it, laughed and threw it back. "Right," he said. "I'm going to take a quick visit to the throne and then I'm outta here!"

"And please don't be late back Alan," Angela instructed. "I want to leave here early this evening to avoid the traffic and get a decent parking spot."

"Yes Ma'am," Alan replied, with a faux salute and headed out of the kitchen. "Hey," he suddenly added, turning back around. "Why don't you use the cash from Billy to get Abby a poster or something from the concert?"

"Oh, I intended to!" Angela replied, with a tone that mildly irritated Alan. It was a tone that reminded him of Rita: Angela's condescending mother. "After all, it is *my* money!"

Alan raised his eyebrows slightly and walked out of the kitchen.

Oh. Your money, is it? He mused, climbing the stairs. *Fine. No problem.*

He entered the bathroom, mumbling to himself as he dropped his trousers and sat down heavily onto the toilet seat. *Well. You can do what you like with yooour money sweetheart. I'll still be pocketing a third of the seventy-five quid that Billy is actually paying for the ticket, so what d'ya think about that? Everyone's a winner at Chez Roberts folks!*

*

21:15hrs. Monday 22nd May 2017.
Fallowfield, Manchester

The cramped bedroom of the small, semi-detached house, looked like any other cramped bedroom in any other small, semi-detached house, but with one major difference.

For the past four days, this particular bedroom had been the hub of a meticulous and lethal project: a project that required skill and patience and the mind-set to believe that God himself had commanded the project be completed. The skinny youth - with poorly grown facial hair and foreboding eyes - may have believed that God had shown him the path to take but in truth, it was extreme religious forces in Syria that had planted that particular belief in his mind and then gone on to teach the radicalised twenty-two year old, British Sunni-Muslim his evil craft.

Dressed in traditional Islamic clothes, the once seemingly normal student - who drank alcohol, smoked weed and was known for nothing more than dropping out of university - was standing in that room, about to begin his *Maghrib Salah*: The Muslim Sunset Prayer.

"Allah-hoo Akbar!" He began; raising his hands up to ear-level … *Allah is great*.

He then recited the first *rakat* (part) of the Maghrib and made himself prostrate before the direction of *Al-Ka'bah*: the most sacred site of Islam, located within the centre of the most important Islamic mosque in Mecca, Saudi Arabia.

"Rabb ighfir lee," he whispered, as he knelt down and then laid his forehead onto the floor. Whether the Lord *would* actually forgive him or not, was a question that would surely be answered before the day was out.

Having finished the third and final part of the Maghrib in obligatory silence, the young man rolled up his prayer mat, sat on his bed and focused on a blue rucksack sitting in the corner of the room. *Tonight*, he thought. *The western world will pay for the lives of Syrian children, murdered by the indiscriminate attacks of America and its allies. Tonight, the infidels will feel the wrath of Allah. Tonight, I will stand before God and he will embrace me for the commitment and the loyalty I have shown in his name.*

A few moments of eerie silence later, the man broke his stare away from the rucksack, checked his watch, and stood up. After putting on a black coat he picked up the rucksack and swung it gently onto his back, adjusting the shoulder straps for a better, more secure fit. He then picked up a small, black box from a desk laden with wires, soldering irons, duck-tape and half-empty packets of nuts and bolts, and studied it carefully. Seemingly satisfied, he placed the box in his pocket and fastened up the front of his coat, cursing slightly when the zip became entangled in the material. Frowning, he held out his hands, studied them, clenched his fists tightly together and opened them out again. Better, but still a little unsteady. He took a deep breath, focused and tried the zipper once again. Success.

In a cracked mirror hanging on the bedroom wall he caught a reflection of himself and for the briefest of moments, felt a trickle of doubt seeping into his mind. He quickly closed his eyes and recited the first *Kalma*.

"There is only one God." He chanted the Islamic prayer, almost under his breath. "And the prophet Mohammed is his messenger!"

The young man opened his eyes and as expected, the trickle of doubt had miraculously rescinded. Praise be to Allah.

Without another word or thought, the sworn Jihadi of Isis glanced around the room he would never return to and subsequently left the house. His destination: the city centre of Manchester.

*

04:00hrs Tuesday 23rd May 2017

In all of his twenty-four years of service, Detective Chief Superintendent Riley had never witnessed such a horrific scene. He could, of course, recall the IRA bombing of Manchester city centre twenty-one years previously - when he was a young constable - but this? This was different. This was …

The IRA, he thought, had at least given some warning of their intentions and thankfully - with more than a little luck in play - nobody had lost their lives. But not here: not now. This was mass murder, an act of incredible cowardice, believed to have been carried-out by some deranged suicide bomber: a pathetic individual who, in the name of his God, had targeted concertgoers with his twisted mind and homemade explosive device.

"Children for fuck's sake!" He hissed.

"Sorry boss," The Detective Inspector, standing close-by, quizzed. "What was that?"

Riley waved a dismissive hand and sat on his haunches, surveying the carnage from ground level. Hand bags, items of torn clothing and over-priced concert memorabilia lay scattered amongst blood stained rubble, discarded bandages and shrapnel from the blast: a macabre ending to what should have been a safe and enjoyable evening. He took a large intake of breath and sifted aimlessly through the debris by his feet, buying himself some time to fight back his rising emotions. This was the time to stay professional, he thought, and despite what he wanted to say or do, he couldn't - he wouldn't - lose it now.

Riley frowned when something lying in the dust caught his eye. He removed a pen from his inside pocket and used it to pick up the item that served to bring the horror of the evening into sickening perspective.

"What happened to you, *Abby*?" He eventually whispered, before closing his hand around the delicate bracelet and placing it into his pocket.

***

Seven

Alan and Kyle Roberts stood up as the doctor approached them, whilst the youngest of the Roberts family - Michael - remained sleeping across the waiting room chairs. It had been a long night at the Manchester Royal Infirmary, not just for them, but for all the other desperate relatives of concertgoers awaiting news about their loved ones.

The doctor's expression was unreadable; fatigue and the dire situation at hand causing him to switch to autopilot. This was the one part of his job that he hated and despite having delivered the same news to several people during the past twelve hours, he knew that it wouldn't get any easier.

"Mister Roberts?" He asked.

"Yeah, yeah that's me Doctor. What's happening? Are my wife and daughter okay? Have they …" Alan stopped short as the doctor raised his hand.

"Your daughter…" he glanced down at his notes. "… Abby?" He looked back at Alan, who nodded his confirmation. "Abby is stable but still in a very critical condition. She had pieces of shrapnel in her right leg and torso, which we have taken out without any complications, but unfortunately…" The doctor paused for a moment.

"What?" Alan quizzed. "Unfortunately what?"

"Unfortunately," Doctor Rhodes continued. "We had to amputate what little remained of her right hand."

Alan gasped. "Oh my God, oh Jesus!"

Kyle felt himself go cold, his eyes starting to well. "But," his voice quivered. "She'll be okay won't she Doctor? I mean, she's gonna pull through yeah?"

Rhodes managed a faint reassuring smile. "It's early days yet young man but, given Abby's age and the fact that she is responding well to treatment, she should make a good recovery."

Kyle began to sob and, for the first time in a very long time, his father hugged him.

"It'll take time, of course," Rhodes continued. "And a great deal of specialist help but for now, she's in good hands."

Alan patted his son on the back, pulled out of the embrace and smiled at his son. It was a moment of father/son love that sadly neither would replicate ever again. Eventually, Alan turned to face the doctor once more.

"And my wife, Doctor," he asked with a new feeling of hope in his heart. "How's she?"

Rhodes glanced down at his notes for a second time, pretending to search for a patient he already knew the name of.

No. He reflected, dolefully. *This bit doesn't get any easier.*

*

Kyle looked down at his phone as it vibrated for the umpteenth time and pressed the red *reject* button for the umpteenth time. He didn't much feel like talking to anybody right now, least of all Mehmet. Why the fuck was he phoning so much anyway? Was it guilt because his own sister Ecrin had endured nothing but a bad period pain over the last twenty-four hours, whilst lying in the warmth and safety of her own bed? Or was it because he still had a mother, whereas Kyle...?

He's your friend, isn't he? The inner voice reminded him. *Of course he's going to phone you.*

The contemplation to phone Mehmet back was disturbed by a sudden knock on his bedroom door.

"Yeah?" he called out, swinging his legs off the bed and placing his phone onto the bedside cabinet.

It would be another four weeks before Kyle saw or even spoke to Mehmet again, although it would be far from a friendly encounter.

*

Three of the Roberts' siblings sat huddled together in the corner of the Working Men's Club where their mother's wake was being staged; all three of them - as well as their father - were staggered by how many people had actually attended, especially given the poor turnout at Moston Cemetery earlier. Their elder brother - Thomas - was currently serving a prison sentence at HMP Strangeways but had been granted permission to attend his mother's funeral. It was spun as an act of compassion as the Governor knew that if he didn't allow it - which had been his initial decision - the press would have had an almighty field day.

"HMP Strangeways heartless Governor refuses an inmate's plea to say goodbye to his dead mother, killed in the Arena bombing!"

Not the kind of attention a Manchester prison needed amidst the dark of a Manchester tragedy. And so, the Governor had allowed the day release of Thomas Roberts, though his permission most definitely did not extend to allowing the criminal to go to the subsequent wake. Governor Winthrop wasn't that reverent … or stupid.

*

Situated in a part of Manchester where the locals frowned upon anything non-British, the large function room of the club - with adequate bar facilities - had been hired out for free to long-standing member, Alan Roberts.

"It's the least I can do Alan," the Chairman of the club's committee had responded to his patron's gratitude. "Angela was well-thought of by a lot of people around here, all of who will want to pay their last respects. We can rustle up some food - nothing too fancy - but…"

"Sorry Bill," Alan cut in. "I can't really afford to put food…"

Bill quickly held up his hand. "Alan," he said, sternly. "I said that *we* would put some food on, yeah? The committee are behind me one-hundred per cent, so it'll cost you absolutely nothing."

"Bloody hell Bill," Alan's voice cracked with emotion. "I don't know what to say."

"You say *yes* Alan," Bill replied. "And let us all give Ang' a good send off."

Alan had been overwhelmed by the generosity of Bill's offer that day, whereas Bill - sympathetic and kind Bill - had calculated that the takings on beer sales alone would far outweigh the cost of a few sandwiches and cocktail sausages. Nothing better than a funeral to bring on a thirst.

*

"You okay?" Kyle asked, looking at his sister. He knew that she wasn't, sitting there in a wheelchair with more bandages than flesh on show. She had taken tremendous strides on her road to recovery and had been allowed to leave hospital a lot sooner than anybody expected but he also knew that she - like he - would be missing their mum terribly and still trying to make sense of what had happened. What he didn't expect - nor prepare for - was Abby's response to his question.

She looked up and held Kyle in a glassy-eyed stare for a while, as if contemplating the question he had just asked. She then tilted her head slightly to one side and spoke so softly that it was difficult to hear her above the crowd.

"Why do think mum died and not me?" She asked. Kyle felt a sudden chill run throughout his entire body, opened his mouth to speak but found that he couldn't. "Does it mean that she was a bad person?" Abby added

"No Abby," Kyle replied quickly. "You know she wasn't a bad person, you know that. It's just that … well, it's because…"

Because what Kyle? Explain it to your sister!

To both Kyle and Abby's surprise, it was their younger brother Michael that finished Kyle's sentence, with an innocence that neither of them had witnessed in a very long time.

38

"None of them people at the concert were bad Abby," he offered. "It's just that God needed new angels, that's all!"

Abby put her hand onto Michael's and gave it a gentle squeeze whilst Kyle patted him on the back.

Michael looked down at the table and allowed himself a small, contented smile, proud that he had remembered his Head Teacher's words - spoken during the previous morning's school assembly - almost verbatim.

*

Kyle stared into the mirror of the gents' toilets, the strong smell of disinfectant blocks - sitting in the bottom of the stained urinals - almost burning the capillaries of his nostrils. When the entrance door swung open, he glanced sideways into the mirror and saw Danny Steele walking in. Kyle's dad had nicknamed the youth *Steely Dan* - after a band that neither boy had even heard of - many years previously, when Kyle and Danny were fairly close friends. These days, Steely and Kyle barely saw each other, let alone speak.

Danny was a stereotypical, unemployed, inner city youth of eighteen: pissed off with the country he believed owed him a living, yet paid way too much in job seekers allowance for him to actually consider working for it. He had a strong Mancunian accent, a strong love for Manchester United and a strong belief that the Gallagher brothers would get back together and rekindle the *Oasis* magic. With little interest in anything other than football, beer and a more-than-occasional spliff, Danny spent his time watching the *Reds* on Sky Sports or hanging out in his mate's bedsit: a beer or the buzz of marijuana accompanying him respectively. Though his shaven ginger hair, sallow complexion, sunken cheeks and oversized hoodie made Danny look a tad on the scrawny side, his actual physique was well toned thanks to the weights he lifted in his parents' garage-cum-gym. He was also deceptively strong and not afraid of anything or anybody: from speaking his mind - better described as running off his mouth - to battling with somebody twice his size or twice his age. He left school at sixteen, took an apprenticeship as a bricklayer but quit less than four months later when he realised that dark and cold mornings weren't really his thing. Before he was eligible to claim benefits, he made money by taking temporary *cash-in-hand* jobs but remained ever hopeful of the day when a scout from Manchester United would see him playing Sunday League football and sign him up post haste … a dream that so many disillusioned, *ne'er-to-be-spotted* Sunday League football players have.

Saturday nights in the North Manchester Working Men's' Club - where he found himself now - were normally where and when the football team meetings took place, meetings that usually consisted of the next day's kick-off time and names of the starting squad, followed by a lot of beer. Bill Roper - club Chairman and team Manager - had pre-warned the lads the previous week, that a wake was being held that Saturday night in honour of Angela Roberts and that they were ALL obliged to attend. Nobody in the team objected especially given how the born and bred Manchester woman had met her demise. A terrible affair.

Danny had - by his standards - made an effort with his appearance for the wake of a once-close friend's mum: he'd washed and ironed both his jeans and his white football shirt as a mark of respect. He'd even given his trainers a wipe over too, although that particular event had earned him a clip around the ear from his own mum who thoroughly disapproved of using the dishcloth for anything other than dishes.

To Kyle, Danny hadn't changed a bit, although he would never understand why the once-promising football player had sacrificed his amazing skill with a ball by hanging out with the local no-hopers. Life, he considered morosely, seemed to have a funny way of making losers out of people.

"Alright Steely?" Kyle asked, still watching the youth via the mirror.

Danny seemed a little startled, as if he hadn't noticed Kyle was there, which was probably the reason for his stupid reply.

"Alright Kye, how're things?"

"How do you think?"

"Aw shit, sorry mate … fuck … I didn't mean …"

"It's alright man," Kyle interjected, sparing the awkward youth any more embarrassment. "Thanks for coming though mate, it's really appreciated."

"Nah, no worries mate. Your mam was a nice lady, everyone thought so."

"Cheers Steely."

"Fuckin' disgraceful what happened though."

"Yeah."

"I mean, what sort of chance did any of those people have? None mate, absolutely none."

Kyle didn't respond.

"And how the fuck does some Paki cunt just walk through security with a bomb strapped to him? It just doesn't make any sense man."

41

"I don't think he was a Pakistani, Steely." Kyle tried, which appeared to confuse Dan.

"What? Well, maybe not a Paki but defo one of them Muslim fuckers. All the same to me mate. Stink like shit and 'ate the fuckin' white race!" Dan buttoned up his flies and went to stand by the washbasin next to Kyle. "Your old man was telling me how your sister's mate should have been at the concert but suddenly developed some mystery illness and couldn't go."

"He said that?" Kyle asked with a frown.

"Yeah," Danny continued. "He was talking to me and the lads about it. Bit fuckin' strange that, her being Muslim an' all!"

"What?" Kyle coughed. "She couldn't help being ill Steely. It was just one of those things."

"Nah, fuck that Kye, I don't believe in coincidences. I reckon her family knew what was gonna happen and kept her home. They're all in each other's pockets them fuckers, trust me!"

Kyle was completely lost for words, disgust and disbelief at what was being suggested, consuming every fibre of his body. He wondered when the morals of his once-close friend had manifested into such hatred but more importantly, why his own father had seemingly evoked the conversation in the first place. The evil work of one radicalised Muslim didn't mean that all Muslims were of the same ilk, just as all Catholics didn't eat fish on a Friday. Kyle didn't like the tone of the conversation that he was becoming engaged in but was utterly shocked by Danny's next comment.

"It's time we started fighting back," Steely began. "And show these greasy fuckers that we ain't gonna roll over and let them take our country."

42

"I don't think that's the answer Dan," Kyle tried, but it was apparent that Dan was now talking to himself and not listening to - or acknowledging - anybody else in that room.

"Maybe me and the boys need to visit *Little Miss Sick*'s house and ask a few questions of our own? Yeah, that's what we need to do, defo. I'm not a religious man but *an eye for an eye* seems like a fuckin' great idea to me right now. What d'you say Kye?" Danny turned around just as the door to the gent's toilets was closing, frowned slightly and shrugged. He then turned back and looked into the mirror, glancing at the three lions on his t-shirt. Standing to attention, he placed his right hand over the England Teams' emblem and began to sing the National Anthem.

Outside of the club, Kyle was urgently dialling a number on his mobile phone for the third time in less than a minute and for the third time the call was diverted to voicemail. He then opted for a text message.

CALL ME ASAP. K

He pressed send and prayed that Mehmet would see it ... sooner rather than later.

***

Eight

In the pocket of a coat that wasn't being worn - hanging in a home that was currently occupied by a mother and her daughter - a phone vibrated for the final time; the display screen showed a number of missed calls and the arrival of a new text message.

In a nearby Mosque, a father and son were listening to the words of the Iman (the Muslim community leader) who was calling for vigilance during these troubled times.

"The citizens of Manchester - and indeed, the nation - are still very much in a state of shock and disbelief over the recent tragedy at the Arena," he said, sombrely. "In our prayers, we must beseech Allah to give them the strength to overcome their pain and suffering. We must continue to stand by them, help them in any way we can and reinforce the fact that such evil deeds are not what the Quran teaches us, nor are they condoned by the true followers of Islam."

Only a minority of heads nodded in agreement, which didn't go unnoticed by the Iman. He knew that the congregation before him were living in fear: fear of reprisals from the ignorant who chose to believe that Muslims directed the attack, not just at white people but at children too. There was no logical reasoning in that belief - no willingness to listen or learn - just a powder cake of prejudice mixed with anger.

"But," he went on. "Whilst I encourage you to stand by those citizens - embrace their sadness, share their pain - you must all remain aware of the fact that vengeance against Muslims in general may be sought by…"

"*May* be sought?" a voice suddenly interrupted, causing a sea of heads to turn towards the source. "With great respect, have our brothers not already been victims of senseless retribution? Mosques have been set fire to in Birmingham and London, and our neighbouring Mosque in Salford has been covered with racist graffiti and damaged by bricks!"

This time, the majority of heads in the room nodded their agreement.

"I have had dog faeces smeared all over my shop window!" A different voice cried out.

"Yes. And I have had my car damaged more than once!" Another added. "How long before one of us or our families become targets?"

There was a ripple of assent throughout the room.

"What are the Police doing to ensure *our* safety Iman?" Yet another voice asked. "Because it seems to me that their hi-visibility presence has waned over the past couple of weeks. We need more than lip service being paid by our protectors!"

The volume of voices in the room grew, as many began to talk about how they - or somebody they knew - had been victimised in one way or another. The Iman waved his hands to bring about order.

"Brothers, brothers, please," he implored, bringing an almost immediate silence to the room. "Let us not spiral into a frenzy of panic. I have been assured by the Chief Constable of the Greater Manchester Police - and by the leader of the City

Council - that measures have been implemented to ensure our safety but…"

"Like what?"

"But," the Iman continued, ignoring the interruption. "We all have to appreciate that police resources are stretched to capacity and we cannot expect a twenty-four hour, personal security service. What we can do is remain vigilant, look out for each other and not take any unnecessary risks."

"Unnecessary risks Iman?"

"Yes. Going out alone at night for example, leaving windows and doors open. Things of that nature."

"So," a voice spat. "We are to be like prisoners in our own homes?"

It was an unexpected and uncharacteristic outburst by Kasim Yilmaz, which took his son Mehmet by surprise.

"Prisoners?" The Iman replied, with a slight smile. "No Kasim, not prisoners. But we *are* Muslims, who need to remain mindful of the … potential … hazards we face, with each and every one of us having a responsibility to safeguard our community. For the time being at least."

"We are honest, hard-working people who pay our taxes Iman," Kasim retorted. "Yet we are being treated like *we* are the aggressors. Don't we have the right to live our lives freely?"

"I suspect that many victims of the Arena atrocity will be thinking the exact same thing Kasim," the Iman responded. "Especially the families of those whose, *right to live freely,* was so cruelly snatched away from them?"

Kasim bowed his head, a little ashamed of his outburst as he remembered how his own daughter had narrowly missed becoming a victim herself. *But, he thought bitterly, have we, as Muslims, not always been victims?*

As the Iman brought the prayer meeting to a close, Kasim raised his head and saw Mehmet staring directly at him, his expression seemingly frozen by a look of deep worry.

"It's okay Mehmet," he reassured his son with a slight smile. "We'll be fine."

Mehmet nodded his head as the congregation rose to leave the mosque but neither father nor son truly believed Kasim's words.

*

"And that's all he had to say?" Azra Yilmaz asked her husband, with a bitter tone. "Keep yourselves locked in and your wits about you? What a wonderful piece of advice from such a revered and supposedly clever man!"

"Azra," Kasim tried, opening his arms and moving towards her.

"No Kasim," his wife cut in, stepping away. "Don't try to pacify me by justifying his shallow words of advice, it won't work. The way I see it, we live in a city that right now, has a hatred for Muslims, regardless of where those Muslims come from. And unless we take steps to ensure our safety now, we will become like sitting dogs!"

"Ducks," Kasim corrected with a slight smile, trying to lighten the mood.

Azra scowled at her husband. "Make a joke if you like Kasim but I'm serious and…" she suddenly stopped and looked over her husband's shoulder.

Kasim turned round and saw Mehmet standing in the doorway looking as though he had just seen a ghost.

"Mehmet?" he asked. "What is it son? What's wrong?"

Mehmet looked directly at his father and slowly held up a mobile phone that was clenched in his hand. It was as though this action alone would miraculously reveal the conversation he had just had with his friend Kyle, causing him to paraphrase the overall content.

"We need to leave Manchester!" Is all his parents initially learned.

*

Sunday mornings were normally reserved for one of two things in the Steele household: sleeping in late, whilst recovering from the previous night's drinking session or, playing Sunday League football; whilst recovering from the previous night's drinking session. This particular Sunday morning however, was going to be very different from the norm. Today was about getting up early, getting your shit together - with the help of a joint - and meeting a few of the lads down at Macky D's.

The *Breakfast Club* - arranged the night before, whilst at Angela Roberts' wake - would consist of Danny Steele, obviously, Malcolm Devlin (Mally), his older sibling Owen (OD) - so called, not because of his name, but because of an incident that involved way too much alcohol and way too much *sniff* - and finally, Jamie Harris aka Wing Nut, due to his large, protruding ears.

A couple of years older than the rest of the group, Wing Nut was the only one amongst them who could drive … legally, at least … and the only one who had access to a van: a past-its-best Ford Transit in a faded, deep red, owned by his current employer, Big Dave. Once a part of the Post Office's fleet of vehicles, the van looked a lot worse than it ran and it ran pretty badly. The bright *Royal Mail* decals - that had once been applied to the side panels and rear door by its previous owner - had long since been removed, leaving a ghost-like impression of letters in the paintwork. Hand-painted over this - though clearly not by an expert in calligraphy - were the words *Big Dave's Removals: No job too much?* By the time that some smart arse had pointed out to Big Dave that the question mark at the end of his well-thought-out slogan should have been an exclamation mark, the enamel paint had already dried solid.

"So what?" Big Dave had responded bitterly. "It's about graft, not fuckin' grammar … *exclamation mark*!"

It was Big Dave's *air* quotation marks, made with his shovel hands and one missing index finger that almost caused a ripple of laughter amongst his listeners … almost. Nobody dared laugh at Big Dave unless he was telling a joke.

*

"You gonna eat that?" Wing Nut asked, pointing at a hash brown in front of Mally.

"Fuck me Wing Nut," Mally replied in disbelief. "Do you ever stop eatin'?" He slid the tray over to his friend, who picked up the item of food from it with a satisfied grin.

49

"There are kids starving in Africa that would kill for this small morsel of goodness," he pointed out, waving the hash brown in front of him.

"Then post it to them, wanker."

Wing Nut looked carefully at the hash brown as though actually considering this option. "Nah, fuck that!" He eventually said, before greedily forcing the whole piece of fried, grated potato into his mouth.

"Yeah, dint think so," Mally smiled, flicking a screwed up *Egg McMuffin* wrapper towards his best mate.

"Right," Danny started. "Let's fuck off and do what we need to do, yeah?"

The rest of the group nodded their agreement, followed Danny out of the otherwise deserted restaurant and piled into the van.

Their brief that morning had been simple. Visit as many local mosques as they could - identified by Wing Nut's smartphone mapping system - and express their thoughts and feelings all over the brickwork using spray paint unwittingly provided by Big Dave. It was time to start a mini revolution in the memory of those lives lost in the Arena tragedy and if any brave fucker wanted to try and stop them, then they'd better have an army with them.

As the van trundled down the quiet road heading towards its first destination, Danny looked out of the passenger door window and scowled.

"Fuck me!" he suddenly spat, causing the crew members sitting in the rear of the van to look up and frown.

"What is it?" OD quizzed, leaning forward. "What you seen man?"

"Quick, spin the van around Wing Nut," Danny continued excitably "I think we may have found ourselves a little bonus!"

*

"What about these?" Ezra asked, holding up a shoebox full of various money-off coupons.

"No Ezra," her mother shot back. "Just the essentials!" She immediately regretted snapping at her daughter, especially given the look of hurt on the teenager's face. "Oh, Ezra," she offered, quickly embracing her daughter. "I'm so, so sorry. I didn't mean…"

"I know mum," Ezra cut in. "It's okay. Really."

"I'm lucky to have you," Azra said softly, stroking her daughter's hair. She then kissed the top of her head before turning away, hoping that her daughter wouldn't see the tears falling.

Ezra had, but said nothing.

She also didn't consider herself to be very lucky. Her best friend Abby had lost her mum at that concert and been badly injured herself. And now, because of the ignorance of a few, Ezra and her family were being forced to run from their home and hide because nobody cared enough to ensure their safety. *Luck?* Ezra considered. *Only the bad kind.*

*

Mehmet turned around as his father entered the bedroom and saw the face of a very worried man looking back at him. A forced smile suggested that he was trying to remain calm and positive but Mehmet knew just how far from the truth that was. In fact, over the last ten hours or so, Mehmet was convinced that his father had started to look older than his years.

"You okay son?" Mehmet merely shrugged, non-committedly. "It won't be for long," Kasim went on. "And we will be a lot safer living with your aunty for now."

"But how long will we have to stay?" Mehmet asked. "Everyone we know and everything we have is here … in Manchester … in this community."

"I know this," Kasim tried. "And had it not been for your friend pre-warning us, we …"

"Maybe it'll blow over," Mehmet cut in. "Maybe he … *we* … are over-reacting to the words of a drunken idiot?"

"Mehmet…"

"And, if anything was going to happen, it would have happened by now…"

"Mehmet, listen…"

"So we should stay and …"

"Mehmet, enough!" Kasim said firmly, stopping his son mid-sentence. "You might think it is a risk worth taking," he went on. "But I'm not prepared to chance this family's well-being based on a *maybe-he-will-maybe-he-won't* attitude."

"So, we run away and hide?" Mehmet snapped. "Like cowards!"

"It has nothing to do with being cowardly," Kasim snapped back. "It's about preservation, not stupidity. We have to make the right decision and put our trust in Allah that …"

"Ha!" Mehmet snorted bitterly. "Trust Allah? It is because of our religion that we are in this mess to start with!"

"Mehmet!" Kasim scolded.

"What?" Mehmet shot back, his lips trembling. "Don't denounce Allah? Don't question, why he has let this happen?"

"Don't disrespect our faith," Kasim replied. "You should be proud of being a Muslim, not …"

"Proud?" Mehmet interrupted. "Why would any Muslim be proud right now? We are all seen as fucking terrorists!"

Mehmet didn't see the hand of his father move but he certainly felt it connect with his cheek as the burn of the slap radiated around the left side of his face.

"I will not have that language in my house!" Kasim snarled. "Do you hear me?"

Mehmet glared at his father, shocked but resolute not to break down in front of him; he wasn't going to let this stubborn man see him cry. He pushed past Kasim and stormed out of the room and down the stairs.

"Mehmet," his father called out, now regretting hitting his son. "Please don't …"

Mehmet had already pulled the front door closed and was walking briskly away from the house before his father had finished the sentence.

Azra appeared at the foot of the stairs and looked up towards her husband. "Kasim?" She asked with a worried expression "What's going on? Why has Mehmet gone out?"

Kasim waved a weary hand at his wife. "It's okay, it's okay," he assured her. "He just needs to get a little air. He'll be back soon."

Or at least, Kasim prayed he would be.

*

Mehmet had no idea where he was headed and in truth, he didn't really care; he just needed to be away from the house for as long as it took the throbbing in his face and the pain in his heart to subside. He had never spoken to his dad like that before but, more importantly, his dad had never hit him before. Deserved? Probably not, but given the degree of insurmountable tension lately, probably not unexpected either.

For fifteen minutes, Mehmet wandered aimlessly around the streets of Cheetham, lost in his own world of troubled thought. He was so distracted that he failed to notice a van pass by and then turn around. He also didn't notice it pull up directly behind him and idle. In fact, the only time he realised it was there at all was when somebody called out his name and made him turn around. Even then he only caught a brief glimpse because something itchy and smelling of rotten fruit was forced over his head. As his vision was banished into darkness, a hard strike to his abdomen took the breath from his lungs.

Thrown into rear of the van, Mehmet felt somebody pull his arms around his back and tie his wrists together, so tightly that the circulation of blood to his fingers ceased almost immediately. He knew he should have felt afraid about what was happening but for some reason, that emotion didn't manifest itself at all. Instead, his only thought was of his family and in particular his dad, who would only blame himself for this ... whatever *this* was.

*

In the pocket of a coat that wasn't being worn - in the bedroom of a house where a young adult usually slept - a phone was vibrating, as it had done for the past one hour and forty-five minutes. This time, it wouldn't get answered.

***

Nine

"But you don't understand," Kasim pleaded to the person on the other end of the phone. "I can't wait for twenty-four hours. His life is in danger and…"

Pause.

"Yes, he has been threatened with violence."

Pause.

"Not directly no, but his friend…"

Pause.

"What does it matter if it's third party or not? The threat…"

Pause.

"Then *I* want to report the threat!" Kasim's voice was starting to rise with anger and frustration.

Pause.

"How can he report it, you stupid woman?" Kasim finally snapped. "The boy is missing, which is what I am trying to tell you. Why aren't you listening to me?"

Pause.

"No, I won't lower my voice, not until I get you to understand how bad this situation is!"

Pause.

Kasim turned to his wife and shook his head in desperation. Why couldn't he get the help he needed? Why was the person on the receiving end of this 999 call being so cold and so difficult and so…?

"No … well, yes … but his phone is here, he didn't take it with him."

Pause.

Azra sat on the couch with her daughter's head across her lap: her heart racing, her eyes unable to stop shedding tears. It had been almost two hours since Mehmet had left the house in anger yet only ten minutes since she had discovered his phone in the pocket of his coat, lying in his bedroom. Her husband had immediately telephoned the Police, reassuring her - in an unconvincing tone - that Mehmet would be fine and the Police would find him soon enough. And whilst she tried to believe that Kasim was right, she was a mother and had an instinct that only mothers close to their offspring possess. For the time being, she would keep that instinct to herself and try to push it to the back of her mind; a difficult thing to do when your breaking heart is a constant reminder of it.

"Okay, yes," Kasim continued on the phone, with a little less bitterness. "We can do that but…"

Pause.

"Yes, I understand, thank you. Thank you." Kasim hung up and turned once again to his wife and daughter. "They are on their way," he informed them. "But it could take an hour or so for somebody to get here."

Azra nodded and tried a comforting smile of her own despite her motherly instinct - her subconscious, her heavy heart - telling her that whatever the Police decided to say, do or promise, it was already way too late.

Almighty and loving Allah, she prayed silently. *Please let me be wrong!*

***

Ten

The room sweated a bitter odour of damp and rotting wood, though the added stench of animal faeces made it even more difficult to breathe through the heavy material of the sack covering his head. Mehmet knew that he was on the first floor of whatever building he was in as he had literally been dragged up a flight of stairs before being thrown into the room where he now sat, bound to a chair.

Through the pinprick holes of the hessian sacking, Mehmet could see shadows pass across what little light reached his eyes and figured that at least three people were his captors, despite him only hearing one voice. It was the same voice that had called out his name whilst he was walking along the street earlier, the same voice that had told him to stop struggling or things would get a lot worse. How much worse could things get? Mehmet had thought - almost comically - when a hard fist had unexpectedly made contact with his jaw. There was a moment - in the shock and confusion of it all - that Mehmet had actually contemplated correcting the owner of the aggressive vocal chords by pointing out that he wasn't in fact a *Paki cunt,* nor was he any other sort of cunt for that matter. Wisely, he'd surmised that any sort of retort might not have been his best move of the day, so chose to remain silent.

The voice had given instructions to the other parties present: *Sit him down. Tie him with this. Make sure it's tight, we don't want our guest leaving too fucking soon, do we boys?* And then, with a couple of taps from an invisible hand on his covered cheek, the voice had told him to sit tight, as they would be back before he knew it. *Can't wait*, Mehmet had thought with unusual and inappropriate mirth.

From the blast of cold air that occasionally swept across the back of his neck, Mehmet guessed that a window in the room was either open or broken, the latter being favoured as he had heard the crunching of glass beneath somebody's feet. This, he considered, might be in his favour. If he could somehow manage to get a shard of glass into his hands, he could cut the rope and …

Wait a minute. He checked himself with an obvious yet overlooked afterthought. *They haven't gagged me.*

"Hel…" he tried to call out, but his dry mouth and aching jaw prevented his intended plea from sounding anything other than a croak. He ran his tongue around his mouth to evoke the secretion of saliva, before moistening his lips and attempting to call out for a second time.

"Help!" Not perfect but better than before. "Please … anybody … I need help!"

The whisper of the wind humming through the broken glass of the window was momentarily drowned out by the distant bark of a dog but other than that, he heard nothing.

"Somebody help me …please!!"

Although this attempt was much louder than the last, it seemed that only some far-off canine with sensitive ears could hear him. However, after a few cursory barks even the dog lost interest and Mehmet resigned himself to the fact that nobody was coming. He exhaled a long, warm breath, dropped his head and closed his eyes.

*

"What's wrong with you?" Alan asked his son. "You're acting like you got fleas up your arse."

Kyle looked up from his barely-eaten breakfast cereal and frowned. "What did you say to Danny last night?" He suddenly asked.

"Danny who?" Alan replied, with a wry smile.

"You know which fucking Danny I mean!" Kyle snapped.

"Whereas you seem to have forgotten who you're talking to!" Alan growled; the smile gone. "I'm not one of those Muppets you hang around with Kyle, so watch your mouth!"

"But you don't mind talking to one of those Muppets and filling his head with crap?"

"I didn't fill Steely's head with nothing."

"So you know which Danny I'm talking about then?" Kyle muttered, sarcastically.

"Don't be a smart-arse Kyle. Of course I knew who you meant, I was just havin' a bit of a laugh with you, that's all … Jesus!"

"But it's not a laugh dad, Danny's a fuckin' psycho and now he's got it in for Mehmet because of you!"

"Because of me? What the hell have I done?" Alan challenged.

Kyle shook his head and stood up. "It doesn't matter," he sighed, heading for the door. "I need to go find Mehmet before Danny does."

"Hang on a minute" Alan called out with a foreboding tone, making Kyle stop and look back. "Why are you making such a big deal about it?" Kyle opened his mouth to speak but closed it again. "I don't get it." Alan continued. "Why do you give a monkey's toss about what happens to one of them lot?"

"One of *them lot*?" Kyle repeated bitterly. "What does that mean? Pakis? Muslims? Fucking terrorists? Which one of *them lot* are you talking about … Alan?"

The defensive retort by Kyle didn't bother Alan so much; it was his son's cold use of his forename that unexpectedly hurt. This time, it was Alan who opened his mouth to speak but closed it again, still on the back foot.

"For one thing," Kyle went on. "Mehmet isn't Pakistani, he's half Turkish, and for another, he's my best mate!" Kyle frowned, realising what he had just said and immediately regretted the fact that he himself hadn't acted more like a best mate.

"Aw, isn't that nice?" Alan cut in with a skit. "Sticking up for your little Muslim friend. Am I okay to say that, or is that not allowed in my own country either?"

"You're pathetic," Kyle spat.

"Me pathetic?" Alan hit back, his face reddening with rage. "Have you forgotten who we buried yesterday because of those fucking Muslims?"

"That's not …"

"Or what state your sister is in right now? You're a selfish little twat Kyle, you always have been. And don't start giving me the crap that Mehmet knew nothing about it. They all did, with their secret fucking networks and mosque meetings!"

"Jesus!" Kyle hissed, with a faux smirk. "You really are a bigger nob head than I thought!"

As the red mist quickly consumed Alan, he advanced towards Kyle; fists clenched, his face contorted with a snarl. In one swift movement, a well-targeted punch was thrown. Hard knuckles connected so solidly with the bridge of his nose that

61

the sickening snap of bone was audible to both parties. And, as he crashed unceremoniously to the floor, Alan wondered which was worse: the pain to his face or the fact that his son had just hit him.

Kyle wasn't proud of himself. He had never dared strike his dad before and watching him fall to the floor didn't rank as his greatest achievement. What was worse was the look of utter shock on his dad's face as he reeled backwards and dropped to the ground. Still, he wasn't about to stand there and become a punch bag no matter what nurtured respect he had for his parent in the past. Kyle wanted to reach down and help Alan up, to apologise, to make amends but - honestly - what was the point. Instead, he shook his head at the sorry looking heap, turned and walked out of the door.

"Yeah, that's right." Alan called out after him. "You'd better do one, you little prick!" Kyle closed the door quietly behind him. "And don't bother coming back into my house!" Alan shouted. "Do you 'ear me Kyle? … Kyle?"

Kyle stood outside for a moment, listening, contemplating his next move. After a few moments he had reached a decision. He took a deep breath, dabbed his eyes and set off quickly down the garden path. Right now, finding his friend was way more important than the rants of an embarrassed man. He knew that it was probably too late to start acting like a best friend but he prayed that it wasn't too late to find one.

***

Eleven

Kyle sat staring at the floor trying hard not to list, as the worn springs of the couch he was sitting on offered little support under his weight. He could feel the top of his head almost burning from the intense stare from another pair of eyes in the room and actually considered leaving. He probably would have too if Mrs Yilmaz hadn't come back into the room, carrying a tray of tea-filled cups. *Tea,* he mentally scoffed, taking a cup from the tray with a polite smile. *Why do people think that tea will make everything all right?*

Kyle blew, and then sipped the tea, grimacing slightly at the weak and unsweetened taste. He didn't complain though, as he reckoned that - given Mr Yilmaz's mood - he'd have been wearing it if he did.

*

When Kyle had left his home earlier, he'd immediately made his way to Mehmet's house hoping that his friend would be there. However, when the front door was opened, Mr Yilmaz's instant tirade left him in no doubt that Mehmet wasn't.

"What are you doing here? Have you any idea what you have done? You have scared my family half to death with your *friendly concern* and now, Mehmet is missing. Do you know where he is?"

"No, I…"

"Then what use are you to me? I want you to leave and pray that my son returns unharmed or,

63

upon my life and the lives of my family, it is *I* that will come looking for *you*!"

"Kasim!" The stern voice of his wife called out from behind him. "This is not Kyle's fault." Azra came forward, casting a disapproving look at Kasim before beckoning Kyle with a soft smile. "Come in Kyle," she continued. "Please?"

Kyle wanted to walk away but the desperate tone of Azra's voice compelled him to reconsider. After a moment's hesitation and a cursory glance at Kasim, he reluctantly entered the house.

*

Once the tea serving ritual was complete, Azra sat next to Kyle and looked at him with a strained smile. Kyle noticed how, in the shortest of time, Mehmet's mum had begun to look old. He had always considered her to be *well fit* - an inner city terminology of endearment meaning *to be attractive* - but now, with her head wrapped tightly and uncharacteristically in a black hijab, she looked tired and aged.

"Mehmet walked out this morning and ... well, he still hasn't returned." She saw the quizzical expression that fell across Kyle's face and instinctively knew that he also found it unusual behaviour for Mehmet. "There was…" She paused and cast her eyes towards her husband, as if what she was about to say shouldn't be shared. Kasim was staring into his cup, as though his mind was somewhere else. "There was a difference of opinion between Mehmet and his father," she continued. "And I just think that, plus the worry of what your friends might…"

64

"Hang on a minute," Kyle cut in defensively. "They're not *my* friends Mrs Yilmaz, I just know them!"

"Yet they seek retribution on your behalf?" Kasim suddenly shot, with a doubtful tone. "That doesn't sound like something anyone would do, unless they were close to you!"

"I swear on my life Mister Yilmaz," Kyle replied. "I only know them because we went to the same school and they live close to me and sometimes, my mum and dad spoke to theirs'. It was my older brother that hung around with them but he's not me is he? And I'm not the one in prison!"

Azra looked across at Kasim as he silently considered what Kyle had said. She had inadvertently used the wrong term when she said *friends* and was prepared to admit it: but Kasim? He mightn't be so accommodating.

"Mister Yilmaz," Kyle continued, anxiously. "Mehmet has been my best mate for years, you know that, so why would I want anything bad to happen to him?"

"Because you think like they do," Kasim growled, gesturing towards the window and the outside world with a flick of his head. "And like them, you blame *all* Muslims of the world for what happened at the arena. That's why we and all the other innocent Muslims of Manchester have become easy targets for shallow minded fools to seek vengeance!"

Something inside Kyle snapped, causing a wave of anger and emotion to rise like bile in his throat. "Innocent?" He spat. "My mum and sister were innocent, Mister Yilmaz, just like all those other innocent people who got killed or injured at the concert. I lost my mum. Who the fuck did you lose?"

"Remember who's home you are in!" Kasim warned angrily.

Kyle shot up. "Then maybe I shouldn't be here?"

"I think you're right," Kasim replied.

"Kasim!" Azra snapped, casting a disapproving look towards her husband before turning back to face Kyle. "Please, Kyle, don't leave. Not like this."

"I'm sorry Mrs Yilmaz," Kyle said quietly. "I came here because I was worried about Mehmet not to be accused of being a racist."

"Oh, he didn't mean…"

"Yeah, he did," Kyle cut in. "But that's okay Mrs Yilmaz. And I'm sorry for swearing, I really am."

Azra reached out and took Kyle's hand in hers, giving it a gently squeeze. "I know you are," she said softly. "Please, won't you sit back down?"

Kyle shook his head. "I'm sorry but I need to go. I have to try and find Mehmet, not sit here listening to…" He suddenly broke off, sighed and looked directly at Kasim. "I don't care what religion the bloke who killed my mum and disabled my sister was Mister Yilmaz because it won't bring them back. But I do care about what happens to my friend because of *his* religion."

Kasim bowed his head slightly. By judging Kyle the way that he had, made him no better than the people who were judging Muslims and that made him feel ashamed. He stood up and faced Kyle. "No," he began in earnest. "It is I that must apologise." He held out his hand to Kyle. "Please forgive me?"

66

Kyle took Kasim's hand without hesitation. He knew that people said and did things that they didn't really mean when they were angry or upset; God knows, he had. "It's okay Mister Yilmaz," he said.

"I'm just so worried about Mehmet," Kasim continued. "He's never done this before. It's so out of character."

Kyle nodded his agreement, not wanting to point out that actually, Mehmet had walked out in anger a year ago because of an argument with his dad. He had been AWOL for a day and a half on that occasion, staying at Kyle's home until he had calmed down enough to go home. Kyle only hoped that Mehmet had gone off in a sulk once again and would return later with his tail in between his legs. But with that hope came an unmistakeable instinct.

And that instinct wasn't good.

***

Twelve

"This piece of crap is going through the fuckin' window in a minute!"

Wing Nut looked up from the bag of wires he was sorting through and frowned. "Give it 'ere man," he said, holding out his hand.

"Be my guest," Mally passed the item over. "But trust me, it's a bag of shit!"

Wing Nut studied it for a moment and then raised his eyebrows in disbelief. "You're such a nob at times Malcolm," he sighed, shaking his head.

Mally hated it when Wing Nut called him Malcolm. It always sounded like his mum was chastising him for swearing or leaving dirty dishes in the sink. Equally though, Wing Nut hated …

"Oh really, *James*," he replied, accentuating the Christian name. "That makes two of us then."

"Maybe," Wing Nut retorted. "But at least I can put a fucking battery in the right way round!"

He pressed and held a small red button making the video camera whirr, then flicker into life. An image of the bag he had been routing through moments earlier appeared on the small screen; not a high-definition picture but adequate enough for what it was needed for. Wing Nut raised the camera towards Mally, asking him to smile.

"For fuck's sake," Mally snapped, quickly shielding his face. "Turn it off y'prick, turn it off!"

Wing Nut let out a chuckle but kept the lens pointed at his friend. "Calm down man," he said. "It's not even recording."

"I don't even care," Mally spat, turning his back towards the video camera. "They can hack into its memory y'know, and bring up whatever's been looked at in the camera's entire fuckin' history!"

"Your mam's tits are gonna be well famous then?" Wing Nut laughed.

"Piss off you dick 'ed, I'm being serious. They have specialist equipment for capturing all sorts of shit!"

They - as far as Mally was concerned - were anybody from Benefit Office investigators right up to the covert operatives of MI5. And he knew it to be true because he'd seen it on Sky … or Facebook … or wherever. He was awash with various conspiracy theories and probably the only one in the Breakfast Club who didn't want to get involved with the current, updated plan. Spraying a few insults on mosques was one thing, but kidnapping? That was some serious shit right there. Still, he held his tongue and stayed involved, but only because he didn't want to look like a pussy in front of his brother or Danny: especially Danny, whose moods were unpredictable at the best of times.

"Okay, okay, it's off," Wing Nut said, passing the camera back. "Look."

Mally glanced at the darkened screen and then snapped it shut. Without another word, he kept his head down, turning the camera round and round in his hands with no particular purpose.

"What's up?" Wing Nut asked, knowing that something was on his friend's mind.

Despite the age difference, Jamie and Malcolm had been the best of friends since childhood and they had come to know each other's traits and emotional *tells* as if they were their own; and this haphazard fidgeting of Mally's was definitely one of those tells.

Mally shrugged his shoulders but kept his head down, staring at the video camera. Jamie didn't break the silence that followed because he knew that Mally would, once he had considered what he wanted to say. He looked like a child, wondering how best to answer a parental accusation when the route of *honesty is the best policy* had failed him so many times in the past.

"What are we doing man?" he finally said. "With that lad I mean?" He looked up at Wing Nut who opened his mouth to speak but was stopped in his tracks. "What do you think Danny wants to do with him, apart from all this shit?" He gestured towards the electronic equipment spewed across the floor. "'Cause I'll tell you what Wing Nut, Danny isn't all …"

"Danny isn't all what?" a voice suddenly interjected from the doorway of the room, making both Mally and Wing Nut jump.

Mally reddened slightly, putting his head down again whilst Wing Nut shot to his feet.

"Fuck me Danny," he gasped. "You scared the shit out of me!"

Danny glanced at him for a short, uncomfortable moment before turning his head back to face Mally again. "C'mon then bro'," he said, with a stony tone. "What *am-ma not*?"

"Nah," Wing Nut tried. "He was jus' sayin' …"

"Shut up Wing Nut," Danny spat, not moving his eyes from Mally. "I'm askin' him, not you! Well Mally? What's on your mind bro'?"

Mally could feel his heart beating faster as the adrenaline began pumping around his body. He knew that Danny wouldn't let this go and unless he came up with something - anything - Danny would lose his rag and start punching. That's what Danny did. That's all that Danny knew. He was a fucking psycho. Not only that, but his regular weed smoking sessions had made him seriously paranoid at the best of times, and this was definitely not the best of times.

But then came a glimmer of redemption.

"What's goin' on?" A newcomer asked.

Hearing the voice of his elder brother brought a sudden wave of relief to Mally's growing angst: not a massive wave, but one that was big enough to make him look up again and regain a little confidence.

"Looks like your little brother has something to say OD," Danny replied, nodding towards Mally. "Int that right mate?"

"What's up our kid?" OD asked with genuine concern.

Mally flicked his eyes between his brother and Danny, suddenly realising how dry his mouth had become and how much his palms - wrapped tightly around the camcorder - were sweating. He swallowed hard and dug deep. "What exactly are we going to do with Mehmet?" he asked. "I mean, what's gonna be the end result? 'Cause the way I see it, once we let him go he's gonna go straight to the dibble and I'm already on my final warning and I don't wanna go to Strangeways but that's where we are all gonna end up and what the fuck is mum gonna think 'cause she's not well as it is and this will …"

"Whoa whoa man!" OD cut in, stepping towards his brother; a tactical move that placed him in between Mally and Danny. "Take a breath, yeah?"

"You lost your bottle little man?" Danny asked menacingly, attempting to step back in front of OD.

OD quickly put his arm out and stopped Danny's advancement: an action that might have been construed as aggressive had it not been quickly followed up with an element of reason. So, when Danny looked down at OD's arm and back up to OD - with an expression that clearly said: *What the fuck are you doing?* - OD looked right back at him.

"I've got this mate," he said, with a foreboding tone that took Danny by surprise. "He might be acting like a tosser but the Devlins don't lose their bottle man. I'll sort my brother out."

There were a tense few seconds when it felt like Danny would explode but eventually, he nodded his head in agreement. He then looked at Mally and issued a warning that made him feel as though he had regained the authority. Nobody else in the room would have agreed though.

"Sort your head out Mally," he hissed. "Or I will, yeah?" Danny then took a step back and turned to Jamie. "Let's get all this stuff in the van, Wing Nut," he continued. "It's time to go *interview* our boy!"

*

Once Danny had left the room, OD turned and glared at his brother. "What the fuck is wrong with you Mal?"

"This don't feel right bro." Mally's face was contorted with worry. "It's gonna end badly, I know it is!"

OD stared silently at Mally and then let out a long sigh. "Look," he went on, calmly. "Nothing's gonna end badly. All Danny wants is his daily fix of putting some poor fucker in fear and today that happens to be Mehmet. Once he has …"

"This ain't about bullying some lad because he won't hand over his *bacci*," Mally cut in. "This is about Danny thinking that every Muslim is a murderer who conspired to blow up white British people and he wants revenge, I know he does!"

"Nah, nah." OD waved his hand dismissively. "It's nothing like that man, trust me. Once Danny has taken the piss a little and shit him up, he'll fuck Mehmet off and move on to his next gripe."

"Why's he videoing it then?" Mally asked. "That ain't normal behaviour bro."

OD let out a stunted laugh. "It's because that's what those Jihadi fucks do to captured soldiers and then stick it all over YouTube."

"What?" Mally gasped. "He's puttin' it on YouTube? What the fuck? That's…"

"Calm down Mal," OD chuckled. "He's not puttin' it anywhere. He's just being dramatic. Underneath that hard-man exterior, Danny wouldn't have the balls to do something like that, or the fucking knowhow. It's just gonna be a few stupid questions and a bit of a laugh, that's all."

Mally looked unconvinced, opened his mouth to say something but quickly shut it again.

"What?" his brother encouraged, frowning. "What's vexing you man?"

Mally looked directly into his brother's eyes with an intensity that OD had never seen before. "This ain't gonna be a *bit of a laugh* bro," he replied sombrely. "This is gonna be a fuckin' trial, with Danny playing Judge and Jury. We need to piss off and we need to piss off now, otherwise…"

73

"Are you sisters ready yet?" Danny's voice suddenly bellowed from somewhere outside the room. "I wanna go to *Gregg's* and get a pasty before we sort the curry-muncher out!"

OD smiled at Mally and laid a reassuring hand on his shoulder. "Everything will be alright mate," he said. "And, if it starts to get out of hand, I'll stop it, yeah?" Mally merely shrugged, still not convinced. "Come on," OD straightened up. "Let's go get some food."

He watched Mally silently gather up the few remaining bits of cable from the floor and put them into a carrier bag. He knew that there was nothing he could say that would put his younger brother's mind at ease but there again, what could he say? There's only a limited amount of reassurance you can truly offer somebody, when you've actually failed to reassure yourself.

***

Thirteen

The vibrating phone rattled annoyingly against the near-empty bottle of sterilised milk it had been left by, its screen flashing intermittently to announce an incoming call. The owner of the phone wasn't too fussed with modern technology and - despite the numerous negative comments from those closest to him - the old Nokia 3310 suited him just fine.

He picked up the mobile, looked at the caller's ID with indifference and accepted the call.

"Yeah?"

"Who's that?" The caller asked, suspiciously.

"Who d'ya think it is, you muppet? You called me!"

"Oh right. It dint sound like you at first. Is everything ..."

"Where are we up to with our little project?" The man cut in, impatiently

"What? Oh, right. All ready this end bro. Just need the director on set, yeah?"

"Did you go where I told you to go?"

"Yeah," the caller replied. *"Though I thought they'd knocked this shit ho...."*

"I'll be there soon." The man cut in again and then terminated the call. This wasn't the time for talking bollocks; this was the time for action, the time for retribution.

*

Danny pulled the phone away from his ear and glared at the screen, chafed that the call had been ended so abruptly. No, *nice work*, *kiss my arse* or nothing.

"Prick," he muttered under his breath, which is where that comment would always remain when it came to insulting this particular bloke.

"Who was that?" A voice behind him asked, making him flinch slightly.

He spun around and faced OD. "What? Oh, nobody. Well, somebody, obviously but…" He suddenly trailed off mid-sentence and appeared to become lost in thought.

"You alright Steely?" OD asked, with a concerned frown.

As quickly as he had drifted off to who knew where, Danny snapped back into the present and smirked at OD. "Yes mate," he replied, waggling his phone in the air. "It's all sorted now."

"What's sorted?" OD asked. "Who was on the phone?"

Danny moved closer to OD and lowered his voice. "Let's just say," he began. "When we came across our little *bonus* this morning, I made a call to somebody who is very keen to meet him in person!"

OD's stomach flipped as the adrenaline of anxiety started to pump around his body. "Mate," he started, glaring at Danny. "Please tell me you didn't call who I think you called?"

Danny's mouthed formed into an odd looking grin as he excitedly nodded his head in confirmation. "Fuckin' right I did bro." He replied.

OD suddenly slumped back against the wall and exhaled a heavy sigh. "What the fuck did you do that for man?" He asked in a low voice of concern.

"We were just supposed to be giving the lad a bit of a scare yeah, but this? Fuck me Steely, you know what will happen if Aaron turns up!"

Danny took another step closer to OD, his smile now lost to a countenance of loathing. "Yes mate I do," he said, tapping a hand against OD's shoulder. "The right fuckin' thing!"

*

Former military Sergeant Aaron Berry - 45 - stood at six-feet-five-inches tall, with every ounce of his eighteen stone frame chiselled in keeping with the proverbial *brick shithouse.*

He had served in the Royal Marines for twelve years - the latter two of those in the Helmand Province of Afghanistan - and had been awarded *The Distinguished Service Cross* in recognition of his bravery during a vicious and bloody confrontation with the Taliban in 2005.

In 2007, he was honourably discharged from the Marines with his Commanding Officer stating that he himself had been proud to serve with Sergeant Berry. Furthermore, he would miss the Sergeant's dedication to the protection of his comrades and the innocent civilians of war-torn Afghanistan and the people of the UK should be proud of his heroic and brave endeavours, both on and off the field of battle. There was nothing more for the Commanding Officer to say, other than to wish Sergeant Berry all the best for the future and that the first round of drinks was on him. Laughter, applause and a heavy session of R&R followed.

In August 2007, Aaron Berry stepped back onto British soil looking forward to a new chapter in his life, a life that would hopefully allow he and his wife of four years - Katie - to start the family they had always talked about. Encouraged by the parting words of his former Commander, Aaron was also expectant of Government recognition for his time spent in hell and assumed that he would be given their full support during the often-difficult transition back into civilian life. Aaron was a proud man when he walked through the arrival doors at Manchester Airport in full ceremonial uniform, and - given the looks of respect and admiration from his fellow countrymen - why shouldn't he be?

Less than a month after his return, Aaron was awoken by a vivid, brutal nightmare; the first of many that were to follow.

Within two years, he had lost his wife through divorce, his physique - and money - through continued drug abuse, and his will to live through the untreated condition of post-traumatic stress disorder.

Within five years of his discharge, former military Sergeant Aaron Berry had been involuntarily sectioned under the Mental Health Act: a decision that was made following a near-successful attempt at ending his own life.

In August 2007, Aaron Berry had stepped back onto British soil looking forward to a new chapter in his life. As it was, he wouldn't have wished that particular chapter on anybody.

*

A year following his incarceration, Aaron was making tremendous progress, partly due to the medication and counselling he was receiving but mainly because of the unwavering and unconditional love of his older sister. She had believed him in, she had sacrificed her time for him and it was from her that he found the strength to push through the wall of depression and find his way back to better days.

Aaron fought with - and defeated - his drug addiction, responded well to therapy and even managed to retrieve most of his former physique. In fact, when he left the Park House Mental Health Facility in the spring of 2014, he had never felt better. Much to the delight of his sister, Aaron agreed to stay with her and her family, just until he got back on his feet. Much to the sorrow of his sister, Aaron moved out less than four weeks later having found a flat and gotten himself a job.

"Well, at least you're only going to be a couple of miles away." His sister had said, trying - without success - not to weep.

"Thank you for everything." Aaron had replied, kissing her on the cheek. "I'll see you soon, yeah?"

As it turned out, hardly a day went by when they didn't see each other. Aaron was happy to let his sister fuss over him and she was happy doing so. After all, looking out for her younger brother? She'd been doing it since they were kids; why stop now?

*

Aaron spent the next two years working as a security officer for *Show Safe*: a company that specialised in the implementation of safety and protection protocols during major events, up and down the country. From concerts to food fares, from marathon races to protest marches, *Show Safe* got involved with them all, often seen as an added string to the Police Services' threadbare bow.

Aaron carried out his role with the same diligence and military precision that he'd used in the Royal Marines; a work ethic that gained him a huge amount of respect from his colleagues and a well-deserved promotion to Event Coordinator. It meant longer hours of course but the position came with a decent pay increase and a company van, plus a few unofficial perks. Aaron very rarely took advantage of the *gratuities* on offer, though he did jump all over the opportunity to get free tickets for an upcoming concert at the Manchester Arena. Not that he would go himself - he hadn't really heard of *Ariana* - but he knew somebody who would.

"Just tell her that you bought them." Aaron suggested to his sister.

"Oh my God. She'll be over the moon," Angela gasped, hugging her brother. "Abby will remember this birthday for the rest of her life, thanks to you!"

***

Fourteen

Aaron may not have been the cause of his sister's death - nor his niece's life-changing injuries - but he certainly felt complicit in it, and there was nothing that anybody could say or do that would change that feeling. After all, had he not given Angela tickets for the concert, he wouldn't have had to watch her coffin slide slowly through a dark velvet curtain to the sound of Eva Cassidy's *Over The Rainbow*. He wouldn't have wondered why - if there was a God - he wasn't the one being laid to rest instead of a good and decent person like his sister. Oh, the priest had spouted on about the Lord moving in mysterious ways and how heaven couldn't have wished for a better soul to enter the celestial gates but, at the end of the day, those were just words. His sister was dead, gone forever and there was nothing on this Earth that could reverse that heart breaking fact. He didn't even have the comfort of being able to call upon his military expertise to track down - and slowly eradicate - the man responsible. And why? Because Salman Abedi had been the mule of destruction, sacrificing himself in the name of Allah. And though some remarked that justice came from Abedi's own death, Aaron strongly disagreed. In his mind, the man was simply a coward who had not only avoided justice but also the burning question of *why* and the subsequent wrath of retribution. To Aaron, the scales of justice had been tipped in favour of the guilty and something was needed to restore the equilibrium. As it was, that particular *something* came along quite unexpectedly.

*

The wake for his sister was full of many familiar faces: those that Angela and Aaron had grown up with - together with their own families - friends old and new, work colleagues and of course, the Parish Priest. Aaron had believed that only a handful of people would attend the wake - given that only a few had turned up for the actual funeral - but the amount of people that came to show their respects was way beyond his expectations. He saw and heard how much the people thought of Angela and he was filled with almost as much pride as he was sorrow … almost.

As the evening drew to a close, most of the gathering had offered their condolences for the umpteenth time and left, leaving just a couple of dozen people to continue raising a glass in Angela's memory. Father Gallagher had fallen asleep in the corner of the room, still holding on to the empty glass that had held several whisky shots throughout the night. Eileen the bar lady - whose excessive make-up couldn't quite mask the aged skin beneath it - had told her co-worker, Brenda, that she was going to wake him up, given that it was Saturday night and all. Brenda - wearing an equal amount of make-up but with far less wrinkles and much larger breasts - reminded her that it was in fact Father O'Leary who would be holding early morning mass the next day and she should let Father G enjoy his nap. Eileen grimaced. She hated it when Brenda called the priest,

Father G. It was disrespectful and highly distasteful … a bit like that ridiculous cleavage of hers.

At the far end of the bar, a small group had gathered, a group of which Aaron was a part. Alan - as pissed as ever - was going on about the state of the country and how, in part, he blamed the do-gooders of the UK for Angela's death. His logic revolved around the lack of control at the borders and how it seemed that anybody with a complexion other than a Briton was allowed to enter the country and roam about freely and unmonitored. The majority of heads in the group were still nodding in agreement when Alan suddenly steered the conversation towards the great spread that had been put on by the club and what a fantastic show of people there had been. He then stared down into his pint glass for a while, momentarily lost in thought. Shaking his head, he finally looked back up at the others within the group and raised his glass.

"To Angela," he toasted, trying not to let his voice break completely.

"To Angela." The group acknowledged, raising their own glasses.

Having regained some composure, Alan talked once again about the tragic events of May 22nd, asking why his wife and daughter didn't have the same luck as Abby's friend and why it was that …

Aaron listened intently and then frowned. Had he misheard what his brother-in-law had just said? He glanced across at Danny - standing next to Alan - whose own look of disbelief confirmed that Aaron's ears were working just fine.

"Hang on a minute," he interrupted, scowling at Alan. "So, this friend of Abby suddenly developed some mystery illness on the night that her favourite pop star is giving a concert? A concert that she had a free ticket for?"

Alan shrugged. "Yeah, that's what…"

"And you don't think that's a little bit coincidental, given that she's a fucking Muslim?"

"What? I … I never really thought about it to be honest." Alan frowned.

"What about now Alan?" Aaron quizzed, bitterly "Now that you *are* thinking about it, what do you suppose might have happened?"

Alan stared blankly at Aaron, the metaphorical penny stuck somewhere before the drop.

"Fuck me Alan," Danny added with a snort. "It ain't fucking rocket science bro!"

"Oh?" Alan snapped, turning to Danny. "Then you explain it to me Steely!"

For a few brief seconds, Danny felt under immense pressure, not completely confident that his thoughts mirrored Aaron's. He could feel his face beginning to redden as all eyes were now on him. He shifted uneasily on his feet and let out an unusual snort.

"Seems to me," he began, with a casual shrug of his shoulders. "Like the girl's family were pre-warned about the attack and stopped little Miss Muslim going to the concert so she wouldn't get mashed by the bomber!"

"Y'see Alan?" Aaron said, turning back to his brother-in-law. "Danny's right. It *ain't* rocket science!"

Alan looked genuinely shocked. It was an outrageous theory. Ecrin was - is - Abby's best friend and they've been that way for many years. She wouldn't knowingly put Abby in any danger, surely to God? But what if Ecrin didn't know and her family did? After all, Alan didn't really know them, other than what Abby and Kyle had said, and that was very little.

Nah, he thought, trying to dismiss the seed of doubt. Ecrin and her brother Mehmet are such polite, well-mannered kids, so it stands to reason that their family are decent people ... doesn't it? But still. It was one hell of a coincidence.

And thus, the raindrops of thought began to water the seed.

"So," Aaron asked, noting the look of realisation on Alan's face. "What the fuck are you going to do about it?"

***

Fifteen

By the time the sound of footsteps could be heard once more, pounding against the bare concrete floor, the day had already faded into early evening. The captive lifted his head when he sensed somebody enter the room he was being held in, walk towards him and stop. Although Mehmet could no longer see any bodily shapes through the weave of the sack over his head, he knew that whoever was there was staring directly at him, studying him perhaps. He also knew that the invisible person was very close, as he could hear the stranger breathing: the only sound in an otherwise unsettling silence.

"Why am I here?" Mehmet suddenly asked. "What do you want with me?"

Silence prevailed.

"Please," he tried again. "What have I done to you? Can't you just let me go? I won't tell anybody about this, I swear. Please let me go. I will do whatever you want."

The entity in the room shifted its position and Mehmet suddenly felt its presence close to his ear, a breath vibrating against the cloth of the sack just before it spoke.

"Can you bring my sister back from the dead?" The voice asked menacingly.

*

"What the fuck do you want, tough guy?" Alan spat, when Kyle unexpectedly entered the kitchen.

Abby and Michael looked up from their crisp-filled sandwiches towards their brother but remained cautiously silent. They instinctively knew that an argument was about to take place because they had both witnessed it so many times before. They also knew how nasty their father could be whenever he decided to drink throughout the day and today was definitely looking like one of those days.

"Where is he?" Kyle demanded, bluntly.

"Abby, Michael, go to your rooms!" Alan instructed his children, without taking his eyes off Kyle. Michael quickly scurried off, not wanting to hear yet another slanging match, whilst Abby remained where she was. "Abby," Alan repeated, looking towards her. "Did you hear me? I said go to your room!"

"No," Abby replied defiantly. "I want to know what is going on with you two?"

"Go to your room, now!" Alan tried again. "Or I'll…"

"Or you'll what?" Abby cut in, bitterly. "Drag your disabled daughter in there yourself?"

Alan opened his mouth to speak but quickly checked himself. His daughter was right. What *was* he going to do if she insisted on staying? For a moment, he felt a little ashamed but the alcohol he had consumed and his son's shit attitude ensured that it was only a *fleeting* moment.

"Oh do what you like then!" He huffed, turning back to look at Kyle.

Kyle scowled at the pathetic looking man before him: unshaven, half-dressed, half-pissed and a nose that had been a hell of a lot smaller earlier in the day. At the time, Kyle had regretted hitting his father

- it's not something you did - but right now, at this very moment in time, he would happily do it again.

"Where is he?" he asked again, taking a step closer to his father.

Out of instinct, Alan stood up quickly - knocking the chair over that he was sitting on - and squared up to his son. "What are you on about?" Alan replied, angrily. "Where's who?"

"Mehmet. Where have they taken Mehmet?"

Alan shrugged. "I don't know what you're on about. Now piss off out of my house!"

"What's going on?" Abby asked worriedly. "And what's Mehmet got to do with anything?" Neither her father nor her brother replied. "Dad? … Kyle? … Why are you looking for Mehmet?"

"You gonna tell your sister what's on your mind tough guy, or what?"

Kyle could feel the rage burning inside. With a temporary loss of the control filter inside his brain, he suddenly lunged forwards, grabbed Alan by the throat and forced him ferociously back against the wall.

"Kyle!" Abby screamed as she looked on in horror.

"Where the fuck is he? Where have they taken him?"

"Kyle, please. Let him go. He's not worth it!"

"Tell me now, or I swear to God I'll fucking end you!"

Like a splash of ice cold water to the face, Alan was partially sobered by the stark realisations that not only was Kyle a lot stronger than he imagined - his attempt at pushing Kyle away had proved futile - but actually, yes; given the heat of this particular scenario, Kyle probably could *end* him. But then again, so what? What good was his existence anyway? His life had all but ended the day that Angela was murdered, snuffed out like a discarded candle with no matches left to reignite the light and the warmth. He would gladly have given up his own life for just five more minutes of the life he had shared with Angela but all he had now were memories; and what good were those when you didn't have anybody to hold at night and share them with? Without Angela, Alan was useless and what made it worse is that he actually knew it. Looking after the home and the kids had been Angela's job and suddenly, he was expected to step in and take over that role? Jesus, he could barely look after himself with any certainty, so how was he expected to deal with a disabled daughter, a son with ADHD and now, this? Alan was angry at the world and everybody in it but he was also completely lost, and that made him sad. And though he never considered it for one moment, it also made him vulnerable; vulnerable to suggestion from those with fewer morals than he, vulnerable to be moulded into the same thought processes as those that had been despised by his wife. And then - in a surreal moment of clarity, with Kyle holding onto his throat and screaming into his face - Alan asked himself the question: *what would Angela say about it all*?

The answer came quickly and without a second thought and though he said nothing, his eyes couldn't hide what his heart and soul now felt. They projected such an intense look of despair and remorse that even Kyle couldn't fail to notice it, quelling his anger with an unexpected grip of pity. He suddenly dropped his arms and stepped back, whilst Alan slid down the wall and lay slumped against it, holding his head in his hands as he wept. Both Abby and Kyle watched on, helplessly. They had never seen their dad like this - not even at their mum's funeral - and it was as foreign a territory to them as it was awkward.

Eventually, Alan took in a deep breath to try and regain some composure, although it wasn't nearly enough to look his son in the eye when he spoke.

"I wanted nothing to do with it,' he began in a low voice, as if answering an unspoken question. "But he just kept going on and on!"

Abby frowned, looked towards her brother and opened her mouth to speak. Kyle quickly held up his hand to stop her and though she glared at him for a moment, shaking her head in confusion and disbelief, she complied with her brother's silent request.

"*What good is it going to do*? I asked him." Alan continued, though more to himself than anybody else. "*It won't bring her back*, I said. *And it won't fix my little girl*, I said. *So what's the actual fucking point?*" He paused to wipe his eyes. "And then Steely jumped on the bandwagon with those little scrotes of his." He went on. "And before you know it, they had this crazy fuckin' idea to…" Alan broke off as though the enormity of that particular *idea* had suddenly just dawned on him. He looked up towards Kyle, the white of his eyes red from tears and alcohol, and shrugged. "What could I do? There was nothing I could have said that was going to stop them from hunting Mehmet or his sister down, so how…"

"What?" Abby gasped loudly. "What do you mean, *hunt them down*? W-what's going on? Will somebody please tell me?"

"Who was it dad?" Kyle asked, ignoring his sister's concern. "Who is the *he* in all this crap?"

Alan dropped his head again. "I wanted nothing to do with it," he repeated. "I was … *am* … angry, yeah. But this?" He shook his head.

"Dad?" Kyle spat. "Who is it?"

After a brief moment of silence, Alan looked back up towards Kyle. "Aaron," he uttered. "It's Aaron."

"Uncle Aaron?" Abby shot in again, with a frown. "What's Uncle Aaron got to do with anything? What the fuck is going on?"

Once more, Kyle ignored his sister's questions, moved towards Alan and crouched down in front of him. "Where was he taking Mehmet dad?"

"I don't know," Alan replied. "I didn't want anything to do with it. Believe me. It's just…!"

"Think dad." Kyle interrupted. "Where do you reckon they would take him? You must have heard something for fuck's sake? Yous lot were all bosom buddies last night. Try to remember yeah?"

Alan continued to shake his head. He couldn't remember getting up this morning let alone the finer details of last night's conversation. He just remembered how Aaron had been, how he had suddenly become obsessed with vengeance and how quickly he had filled the heads of the idiots stood around him with the same evil intent. He recalled, through the mugginess in his head, how Danny (half-jokingly, half-bravado) said something about giving Mehmet a slap and Aaron saying something like: *Why? Did his kind only slap my sister and niece?*

It was a rhetorical question of course but it set the tone of the conversation that followed, which developed from bitter words into a carefully formulated plan; it developed into the conspiracy of a serious fucking crime, is what it did. Alan had wanted to walk away, to tell them that they were all talking out of their drunken arses. He wanted to object, to voice his disapproval but he just sat there and listened; his ability - or strength - to speak out, somehow taken away from him. Consensual by silence, guilty by association.

"Dad?"

The voice of his son snapped him back from his recall and suddenly - from out of nowhere - he remembered something that Aaron had said: a memory he had related to the group about where he and Angela used to play as children and hang out as teenagers. It was a place that Aaron once told Angela had been built in her name and - being six-years-old at the time - she'd believed it.

"Angel Court," he said, as though it should have been obvious all along.

"Angel Court?" Abby repeated, with a frown. "I thought they'd knocked that place down ages ago?"

For the first time since his arrival, Kyle turned and spoke directly to his sister. "There's only one way to find out!"

***

Sixteen

"When was he last seen?"

"About nine o'clock this morning, so almost ten hours ago."

The Detective Inspector frowned. "Fuck me, I've been AWOL in the pub for longer than that. So what's so important that an understaffed CID department has to drop everything to look for this lad?"

"Partly because of the current tension surrounding the Muslim community." The uniformed Sergeant replied.

"And mainly?" The DI probed.

The Sergeant let out a sigh. "Mainly? Because the missing lad's father is a friend of some community leader who just happens to be related to the Super'!"

"Oh, here we fucking go!" The DI spat, throwing down his pen and leaning back into his chair. "Forget the fact that I've got two section 18 assaults to deal with, together with a robbery at knifepoint and a suspected rapist in custody. It's Sunday Chris and I've got two members of staff on duty!"

"I know," Chris replied, shrugging slightly. "But don't shoot the messenger boss. You know what it's like at the minute with everyone shitting themselves about what *could* happen? It'll probably turn out to be nothing - again - but we have to be seen to be doing. You know how it works."

DI Williams let out a discontented breath. He knew exactly how it worked, it was just a pity that it didn't work in favour of somebody who really needed the Police's help. *Another case of who you know and what category of minority you fit into*, he thought bitterly. "All right Chris." He raised his eyebrows. "What else have you got on this *Mehmet* character so far?"

*

By the time the Sergeant had finished his briefing, the DI's attitude towards the incident had changed dramatically. This certainly didn't seem to be a run-of-the-mill *missing from home* and it definitely had the potential to be something more sinister. But the question was, why? Why would a young Turkish lad - with seemingly no involvement in any shit that saturated the area in which he lived - get abducted? ... *Abducted?* Now there's a term that DI Andy Williams didn't use very often, and only then when he was one hundred per cent sure that at least ninety-five per cent of the facts pointed to it being so.

"Right," he said. "Let's re-visit the house and make a thorough search!"

"Yes boss."

"And I mean *thorough* Chris, none of this flicking back the bed covers and glancing in a wardrobe. I take it you've tried ringing him?"

"Well actually boss, he left his phone at home which suggests he wasn't planning on going out for too long."

"Have we seized it?"

"We have but it's locked."

"Okay, get it over to the tech team at Bradford Park and see …"

"Already sorted," Chris interrupted. "But they keep asking for this form and that form and wanting to know, on whose authority is it being sanctioned?"

The DI scowled. *Bureaucracy and red tape*, he thought bitterly. *No wonder the job's fucked.*

He picked up the phone and dialled a private number. He knew that the Chief Superintendent he was about to ring was currently on a rest day - only because he'd been out with him and his wife the night before - but he also knew that Simon wouldn't mind getting this call in the slightest.

"Morning Mr Jackson," Andy said. "I need your help."

Fifteen minutes after Andy had ended the call with Chief Superintendent Simon Jackson, the same phone rang back. Andy answered and listened.

"Brilliant, cheers Simon. I'll phone you later and update you."

Pause.

"Yeah, of course I am, wouldn't miss it!"

Pause.

"Great. Thanks again mate. Catch you later."

DI Williams replaced the receiver and looked across his desk at Chris. "They will have the phone unlocked and ready to collect within the hour!"

***

Seventeen

In the early 1950s - during the post-war building boom of council houses and pre-fabricated high-rise flats to meet the rise and demand of the growing population - Manchester Corporation was proud to stage the official opening of three new high-rise blocks:

"A realised vision of modern, comfortable and affordable homes without the need to sacrifice anymore of the surrounding greenery. These are the future of twentieth century and a clear demonstration of our commitment to the wellbeing and living conditions of the good people within the Miles Platting area and indeed, the whole of Manchester!"...

... or so the words of the local, tape-cutting councillor went.

The speech was met with the appropriate applause - albeit from other councillors and the building company bigwigs - but still, the day had been a moderate success ... politically speaking.

As it turned out, the good people of Miles Platting weren't even offered the chance to move into the new, modern and comfortable flats, as they had already been earmarked to accommodate the overspill from Hattersley council estates; a town that was situated some ten miles south of Miles Platting. Thus, the *locals* were resigned to live in their two-up-two-down homes with no inside toilets and subsequently came to hate the sight of the new flats and - by default - the new occupiers of them.

Just over thirty years later, a large majority of the adults who had seen the flats being officially opened, had been laid to rest, though the disdain for the three *eyesores* never faltered across the succeeding generations. So, in the early 1980s -when it was announced that the flats were to be demolished to: "*make way for the development of modern, comfortable and affordable homes*" - there was local, rejoice. Not because of the promise of urban regeneration but because the three eyesores were finally being razed to the ground. In fact, if some of the long-standing residents of Miles Platting had had their way, then the occupants of said eyesores would have been razed to the ground with them.

By the summer of 1985, only two of the three high-rises had gone. Given the sudden shortage of money - and the fact that the asbestos-filled properties actually cost more to demolish than they had to build - Manchester Council had decided to cease the development until such times as funds became more readily available. The result? A large span of empty land and one lone block of flats left to the hands of nature and vandals. The land became completely overgrown - and a convenient place to burn out stolen cars and dump shopping trolleys - whilst the remaining skeletal structure of the high-rise property became a playground for the local, bored kids with a penchant for smashing glass and spraying graffiti. This area quickly declined from being the fairly tolerable eyesore that it once was to becoming - to quote a colonial expression - *a Scutter's shit tip* (1)

(1) *Scutter* - noun: An Irish slang word meaning runny excrement (diarrhoea) or - when related to or

by the English - a person who doesn't wash, has no job but sits on their stale arse watching Daytime TV all morning. They also drape themselves in cheap gold, imitation clothing brands and refer to their babies as *babbies*.

At the time, only a seventeen-year old girl was slightly saddened by the demise of that last standing high-rise block, but only because her brother - whom she loved so dearly - had once said that it had been built in her honour.

Another thirty years on and that same brother was standing in the lounge of an empty flat in a building that was unfit for human occupation, contemplating his next move. It wasn't irony that had brought this particular brother to Angel Court; it was a twisted sense of vengeance-marred nostalgia.

***

Eighteen

"Do you know who I am?"

"I can't even see you," Mehmet replied. "So how would I know?"

The sudden, hard slap to his right ear not only stung like a bitch but very quickly taught Mehmet that perhaps, sarcasm wasn't the best thing to be using right now.

"Clever little fucker, aren't you Paki?" The voice growled.

"I'm not a P…"

The next slap was equally as hard.

"Shut the fuck up!" The voice commanded. "You are what I say you are and that's the way it's going to be, yeah?"

Mehmet remained silent, only to receive an unexpected yet painful kick to his lower leg. "Aargh! What was…?"

"Did you hear what I said?"

"Yeah," Mehmet spat back, anger rising. "But you told me to shut the fuck up, remember?"

There it was again, a snippet of unnecessary sarcasm. Why was he trying to be such a smart arse? Mehmet braced himself for the inevitable response, courtesy of the man behind the voice but, bizarrely, it never came. Instead, the hessian sack was pulled quickly and roughly off his head causing him to squint in what little daylight was left in the room.

When his vision eventually became focused, he looked at the man leaning against the wall in front of him who, in turn, was glaring back, eagerly biting at something on his finger. Mehmet frowned as his confused mind - still trying to make sense of everything - pointed out that he had never before seen a man gnaw at his fingers with such vigour. He almost asked if he was hungry … almost.

The man spat out whatever he had removed from his now bleeding digit and smiled. "Do you know who I am now?" He asked, almost in a whisper. Mehmet shook his head. "I'm Aaron Berry pal," the man continued. "Ring any bells?"

Mehmet paused for thought but again shook his head. "No, I'm sorry, but I …"

"Okay," Aaron cut in. "Let me give you a little clue. You have a younger sister, yes?"

"Yes, but …"

"And, as far as you know, she's alive and well?"

Mehmet felt a cold shiver run through his body as sudden panic took a hold. "What have you done to her?" he started. "Please don't hurt …"

"Relax, Gupta," Aaron snorted, holding up his hand. "As far as I know, she's fine and dandy!"

Mehmet exhaled a stammered a breath of relief as unannounced tears fell from his eyes.

"Whereas *my* sister," Aaron continued, with almost palpable melancholy. "Well. She isn't so good." He stared blankly into space for a few moments as if he needed to gather his thoughts before carrying on: his thoughts, or his strength. "Y'see, *my* sister is no longer with us because *my* sister is dead!"

"I'm sorry," Mehmet said, in earnest.

"I don't need your sympathy y'little cunt!" Aaron snapped, stepping towards Mehmet. "What I need, is for you to tell me why?"

100

Mehmet flinched. "I…I don't know what you mean. I …"

"Why the fuck is my sister dead when yours is safe and well? What was it? A quiet warning from someone within your close-knit, Paki community?"

"How many times?" Mehmet shouted back, out of fear and anger. "I'm not a *Paki*, I'm Turkish!"

The fist that connected with Mehmet's cheek was hard and exact, striking the cheek just enough to fracture - not break - the bone. Mehmet screamed in agony as Aaron grabbed his hair and forced his head backwards. "How many times Muslim Boy?" Aaron spat. "Don't be a clever little fucker with me!"

"I'm not being, I swear!" Mehmet cried. "But I'm not a Pakistani. I am Muslim, yes, but I'm a Turkish Muslim!"

Aaron laughed coldly and let go of Mehmet's hair. "Ha-ha. Like that makes a difference," he said, stepping backwards. "You're all the fucking same yous lot: sly bastards who hate white people. Well this is my fucking country Gupta and you and all the other Muslims are just guests here, guests that have outstayed their welcome!"

"But … but I don't know what I've done to you. I don't even know you. Please. I think you have the wrong person." Mehmet pleaded.

"Tell me why *your* sister wasn't at the Arena the night when she should've been?"

"What?" Mehmet questioned, frowning with initial confusion. But then - like a lightning bolt sent from Hell - a sense of complete dread struck him as he suddenly realised who the man before him was. "Shit!" He gasped. "You're Kyle's uncle, aren't you?"

Aaron started to clap. "At last, the penny has finally dropped," he cried out, nodding in faux jubilation. "Yes Gupta, I *am* Kyle's uncle!" Aaron continued to nod, fixing his expression with a sinister grin and a piercing glare that made the hairs on the back of Mehmet's neck, stand on end. Though Aaron eventually stopped nodding he continued to stare towards Mehmet, not so much at him but through him … or into him. The silence that followed wasn't as long as it seemed, but to Mehmet - sitting there bound, frightened and in pain - it felt like an eternity.

"His mum was *my* sister," Aaron suddenly continued. "But one of your lot changed that, didn't he Gupta?" Mehmet didn't answer. "And for what exactly?" Aaron went on, regardless. "For Allah? For your so-called, *war against infidels*? Or was it just the promise of seventy-two fucking virgins eager to suck-off a Jihadi Martyr that swayed it?"

"I don't support all that radical crap," Mehmet objected, more strongly than intended. "That's the mentality of extreme fundamentalists, the ones who twist the teachings of the Quran to suit themselves. They're not true Muslims, not in my eyes and not in the eyes of ninety-nine-point-nine per cent of all Muslims for that matter." Aaron remained silent, his expression set as though he was actually listening to Mehmet's reasoning with interest. Mehmet saw this as an opportunity: an opportunity to try and get Aaron to reconsider his actions and set him free. It was worth a shot at least, wasn't it?

"Being a Muslim is not about hate," he went on, carefully. "It's about love and respect and kindness to others, not causing terror or killing people without cause or justification. That's what the Quran is about."

"Hmm." Aaron acknowledged, nodding his head. "Whereas the bible…"

He broke off to the sound of people entering the abandoned flat and turned to face the doorway. Danny walked in followed closely by Wing Nut carrying a tripod with a video camera attached to it.

"Wh…what's that for?" Mehmet asked suspiciously.

"You took your time boys," Aaron ignored the question. "I was beginning to think you had lost your bottle!"

"Nah mate," Danny replied. "Just a few hiccups with that thing." He added, pointing at the camera.

"Lost their bottle for what exactly?" Mehmet tried.

"Set it up over there, yeah?" Aaron directed, paused and then turned back towards Mehmet. "Sorry Gupta," he said. "What were we talking about?" Mehmet opened his mouth to speak, but: "Oh yeah," Aaron went on. "You were telling me about your Muslim book of love and peace and I was just about to tell you about the bible. Y'see Mehmet, my bible … the one that was written by a real God … talks about honouring thy mother and thy father but I'm guessing that that commandment relates to sisters too. It also says - and I'm paraphrasing here - *an eye for an eye and a tooth for a tooth,* which brings us nicely back to your question about the video camera." Mehmet swallowed hard as his ears became filled with the deafening sound of his own heart, racing and beating so hard that he thought it might explode. Aaron moved towards him, leant forward and set his face about six inches away from Mehmet's. "Tonight, my little Muslim man," Aaron uttered with an icy tone. "You are going to become a *YouTube* star. Would you like that?"

"I … I don't … I … what do you mean?"

Aaron smiled a sick smile and placed a hand on Mehmet's shoulder, letting his eyes track the boy's terrified face for a moment. "With our help," he replied, "that video camera is going to record you making your long-awaited journey up to Allah. Y'know? A bit like you fuckers do when you behead a British soldier!" Aaron tapped Mehmet's cheek and stood up straight. "An eye for an eye and all that Gupta!"

Mehmet stared blankly into space, temporarily paralysed with shock. Had he just heard right? Was this psycho actually going to…?

No, no, of course not. Think about it? He's not a murderer is he? He's Kyle's uncle and he's just trying to scare me, isn't he? Venting his sorrow and anger over the loss of his sister, that's all.

Please Allah, let that be all!

***

Nineteen

DI Williams had a very bad feeling about this, an instinct developed over twenty-five years of being in the Greater Manchester Police.

The text messages on the now-unlocked phone of Mehmet Yilmaz - together with the amount of missed calls, registered from the same incoming number - suggested that somebody by the name of *Kyle* had been trying to get hold of Mehmet rather urgently. Ordinarily, the attempted contact might have been construed as this Kyle character trying to check on the welfare of this currently missing person, but most of the missed - or ignored - contact, was made before Yilmaz actually went on his walk about.

Before he considered calling the number that seemingly belonged to Kyle, Williams fired up his computer and logged onto a programme called OPUS (Operational Policing Unit System), designed to search - amongst other things - telephone numbers. If the number had been used to contact the Police in the past, it would have been stored in the intelligence system together with the name and address of the user. If this number *was* recorded and it turned out to be connected to this *Kyle* character, he could then do further checks to see what history was held on both the phone and on Kyle himself. However, given the amount of times that callers change their telephone numbers or use other people's phones to call the cops, this particular search can turn out to be very hit-and-miss with the results it yields. Plus, even if a phone number was used and logged, a lot of those numbers become disconnected over time or just constantly ring out. Furthermore, if the call was initially made from a person with a criminal record, chances are that that phone is just one of a string of phones that they possess. Added to all this, very few people actually answer a call from a *withheld number* nowadays, which is exactly how the Police Service set their outgoing caller id.

Andy wasn't holding his breath as he entered the mobile number and waited for OPUS - or *hopeless*, as it had been aptly nicknamed due to the amount of times it crashed - to complete its search. He watched the search icon spin and let out a heavy sigh, as it seemed to be taking an age to finalise; not a good sign. The Detective Inspector was just about to give up and close the search down when suddenly, the screen image changed and revealed not one, but six results for that particular number. He raised his eyebrows in mild disbelief and clicked on result number one. That - together with the next three results - were merely generic records showing that the phone had been used to call the Police but that no details had been taken down. "What the fuck is the point?" he whispered bitterly, positioning the cursor over result number five and clicking the mouse.

And there it was. An actual incident number to which the phone was linked; albeit an incident that occurred over twelve months ago but still, it was a start. Andy double-clicked on the link.

*

The youth paused at the badly maintained, corrugated steel fence - erected by the City Council a number of years previously - and contemplated the

106

now-faded notice board that hung tentatively by a single screw.

*Dang*er *K*eep *Out!* The remaining red letters warned; advice that hadn't been heeded since the day it was first put up there.

He recalled the time before the fence, when - as a child - he had ventured onto the wasteland and subsequently received a puncture wound to his foot and a tetanus shot to his backside for his troubles, neither of which were very pleasant. Though mum was very concerned for her son at the time, dad merely harped on about how expensive *New Balance* trainers were and how they were most definitely not impervious to penetration by rusty nails.

"A fact that you should remember next time you decide to go and piss about on a dumping ground like a little sewer rat!"

That ten-year-old boy never so much as considered going back onto the wasteland and over the years that followed, he stood firmly by that decision … until now.

This particular stretch of land was hazardous enough to cross during daylight hours, let alone during the onset of dusk as anything from broken glass and razor-sharp scrap metal, to the discarded needles of drug addicts, lurked beneath the dense undergrowth. And, if you were lucky enough not to stand on one of those dangers, you were almost certainly guaranteed to collect a sample of putrid dog-crap on the soles of your shoes. Ordinarily, Kyle wouldn't be concerned with these obstacles because, ordinarily, Kyle wouldn't be walking across this shit-swamp. But today was different. Today it was necessary.

107

He sighed heavily and stepped through a gap in the fence where a panel had been prised off and thrown to the ground. Five hundred yards ahead of him - surrounded by a tangle of bramble bushes, nettles and unkempt shrubs - stood the decaying concrete carcase of Angel Court. The building loomed ominously before him, eerily silhouetted as the remaining steams of daylight disappeared quickly behind it, as though being sucked into an abyss of evil. Kyle shivered and actually considered turning around and walking away.

And he would have done too, had he not seen the faint flicker of light from a first floor window.

*

From the tone and intensity of the knock on the front door, Alan instinctively reckoned that it was either the bailiffs or the Police seeking an audience, neither of which were welcome at the Roberts' home. Alan ignored the first rap and continued staring at the line of empty beer cans on the table in front of him: a line that would continue to grow until he ran out … or passed out.

"Fuck off!" he growled under his breath when the second, more intense knock came.

"Dad!" Abby's irritated voice called out from another room. "Dooooor!!"

Well, thought Alan. *If there was any chance of them thinking that nobody was home and pissing off, there isn't now, is there Abby?*

Alan rose slowly from his chair, feeling the effects of the alcohol as it quickly numbed his legs and spun his head. He steadied himself on the table knocking over a few of the empty cans and - more annoyingly - one that was still half-full. That's when the third, more sustained knock came and that's when he quickly found his balance and stormed towards the door.

"Can you knock any fuckin' louder?" he cursed, as he yanked the door open and scowled at the two men standing on the other side. Alan was immediately surprised to see that it was neither the bailiffs nor the cops that were standing on his doorstep, although he didn't let his expression give that particular emotion away. "Can I help you?" His tone wasn't meant to sound in the least bit helpful.

"Mister Roberts?" the smaller of the two men enquired.

"Who's askin'?" Alan replied, whilst glancing warily at the man's much larger sidekick, wearing an enigmatic smile on his large face.

"Yes, yes of course. So sorry," the smaller man went on. "My name is Kasim Yilmaz and this," he said, holding out his hand towards his companion. "Is my cousin Youssef." Alan didn't speak; Kasim frowned slightly. "I am the father of Mehmet," he went on. "A friend of your son, Kyle?" Alan casually shrugged. "May we come in and speak with you?" Kasim asked.

"You're wasting your time mate," Alan snubbed. "I've no idea where your lad's got to."

Kasim frowned a little. "Then you know he's gone missing?"

Alan realised he had already said too much and that now, there was no way he was going to get rid of these two pissing irritants … *fuck!*

"Well … I … yeah. Kyle mentioned something about it but…"

"Then five minutes of your time is all that I ask sir," Kasim interrupted. "Maybe you will remember something more, once you have a little coffee inside you?"

What? Who the hell is this little fucker, coming to my door and insinuating that I'm pissed? Alan opened his mouth to voice his objection, but the attempt was quickly halted by the unexpected voice of his daughter.

"Good idea," Abby said from behind him. Alan spun around and glared at her, though she merely looked past him towards Kasim. "Hello Mister Yilmaz," she continued softly.

"Oh my dear child," Kasim began in earnest, with an expression of pained sympathy. "I am so, so sorry about your terrible ordeal. I cannot begin to imagine your suffering and grief."

"Thank you Mister Yilmaz," Abby replied. "Please, come in."

A slightly bewildered Alan stepped to one side to let Kasim pass but then had to move backwards to allow the much larger Youssef to enter. Alan closed the door behind them and followed them through to the lounge wondering if perhaps, he should have closed the door from the outside and fucked off. Given his current state though, that action was more appealing than it was possible so he resigned himself to the fact that he would have to listen to what they had to say … as if he didn't already know.

***

Twenty

On the face of it, the Roberts were just one of a number of families in this particular area of Manchester that had had some dealings with the Police in the past, whether that was through reporting a crime or actually being connected to one. There had been a few domestic incidents at the address - linked to the phone number used by *Kyle* - and his parents had had a couple of cautions for public order in the past; nothing to be overly concerned about though. It was only their eldest son Thomas who appeared to be the real bad apple in the crate, as he had a string of theft related offences and was currently serving time in HMP Strangeways for burglary.

And so **- on the face of it** - there was nothing in the *OPUS* record that suggested Kyle Roberts was doing anything other than trying to contact his friend and definitely nothing to raise any suspicion of malice intent. Ordinarily, DI Williams would have benched this line of enquiry or gotten a uniformed constable to have a cursory chat with Kyle at a later stage … ordinarily.

However, Andy spotted something in amongst the report and frowned. He didn't have to click on the incident number that was linked to the Roberts' family file to know what it was about, as it was an incident number he would probably never forget. It related to the terrorist attack at the Manchester Arena on 22nd May and unless the Roberts were terror suspects, there was only one other reason why they would be linked to that terrible incident.

And there it was. Mother, Angela Roberts, a victim listed under the macabre heading of *deceased* whilst her daughter, Abby Roberts, had sustained terrible injuries. It was a horrible set of statistics to be connected to but it caused DI Williams to think outside the box and mull over a possibility; a possibility that was so small, it might have been dismissed immediately. But this possibility was what Williams would refer to as, *an instinctive niggle* and this particular niggle was asking:

Is it coincidence that a Muslim youth has gone missing whilst the son (and brother) of two Arena victims is desperately trying to get hold of him?

Andy Williams didn't believe in coincidences, not in this job.

"Jacko!" he suddenly called out across the room.

The seasoned Detective Constable didn't look up from the *shoot-em-up* game he was playing via his smartphone, but grimaced when he saw his final life being taken by the outlaw, *Black Heart Jake.*

Fuck!

"Yes boss?" he replied, without any real enthusiasm.

"Stop whatever you're doing and come with me." Williams' directed.

"Where we off to boss?" DC Jackson asked, hastily quitting the phone app before gathering up his investigator's kit … *Banner* book, pen, gum, attitude.

"We're going to make a couple of house calls," the Inspector replied. "I've got an itch that needs scratching."

*

It took Kyle a good fifteen minutes to make his way from the boundary fence to what used to be a secure entrance door of the flats, not because of the distance but because of fear: fear at what might have been lurking in the undergrowth, fear of being jumped by some hidden *smack-head* who saw Kyle as his next ticket to a fix, but mainly, fear of what he would discover when - and if - he entered the building itself. What if the light he saw from the first floor window was nothing to do with anything other than it being a squat for *Nasties*?

---

*Nasties (noun): Those dregs of society who - for one reason or another - have chosen to become homeless, exchanging an existence of relative comfort and normality, for a life of substance addiction and hygiene deficiency. Nasties are known to be an aggressive, violent and verbally abusive species that would not hesitate to sell their own mothers for whatever *high* was on offer.

Walking into a den of Nasties, Kyle imagined, would be like offering yourself up as a victim in a Zombie apocalypse; not a pleasant experience. He shivered at the thought but then frowned and shook his head with self-annoyance. "Get a grip bro," he told himself. "You got this." He glanced back over his shoulder, partly to confirm that he was still alone but mainly, to consider if he should go back from

113

whence the fuck he came. The daylight was all but gone but was he going to let his bottle go with it?

Nah, he thought. *Not an option.*

Turning back, Kyle took his first step into the foyer of the building, the sound of glass particles crunching under his foot as though somebody had attached miniature loudspeakers to the little fuckers. Kyle grimaced and stopped immediately, exhaling a long, slow breath as he contemplated his next step. At almost a snail's pace, he edged himself forwards until eventually, he was standing in front of the door to a stairwell that would lead him to the first - and subsequent - floors. Through the partially cracked safety glass of the stairwell door, Kyle saw that it was a lot darker in that area than it was in reality due to a metal security panel that had been fixed across a window adjacent to the steps. He found it slightly ironic that the only thing being kept out by the so-called security panel was natural light. Kyle slowly pushed the door open and was immediately greeted by a rush of cold, putrid air that caused him to gag.

"Jesus!" he hissed, holding up his hands to cover his nose and mouth. The door closed with a gentle *thlop* sound, immediately cutting off the stench. Recovering from the initial assault on his nostrils, Kyle reached into his pocket, pulled out his phone and selected the torch mode. At this time of day, the battery in his phone would have used up most of its charge and Kyle hoped … prayed … that it would hold out long enough to navigate the concrete stairs. Pulling his t-shirt up over his nose, he pushed the door open once again and stepped into the stairwell, the phone held out in front of him.

He swept the beam from side-to-side, looking for any immediate obstacles that would hinder his

114

ascent and then let the light come to rest on something that immediately turned his stomach.

Shit!

Not the shit of any meandering animal - as one might expect - but shit that was most definitely of the human variety. And how did Kyle reach this conclusion? Because, in what appeared to have been a bizarre sense of fucked-up cleanliness, the loose-bowelled culprit, had actually wiped their arse after the act and left the evidential tissue to rot by the side of the fly-ridden stool. What made the whole situation that little bit more fucked-up was the fact that somebody had actually seen it appropriate to profess their pride of this achievement by writing on the wall behind it. *Boland dumped 'ere*, the memorial plaque read, with an arrow of red marker pen pointing down towards the offending mess. Bet Boland's parents would have been really proud too, Kyle thought.

Just then, there was a sound of something crashing onto the floor immediately above him, startling Kyle back into the situation at hand. The hairs on the back of his neck stood on end whilst his heart missed more than one beat. If there was ever a time to run and forget about this madness, then right now was most definitely that time.

***

Twenty-One

"Jesus Wing Nut!" Mally hissed as the tripod holding the video camera fell sideways onto the floor. "If that's broken mate, my dad will go ape-shit!"

"Fuck. Sorry mate, sorry," Wing Nut replied, quickly picking up the equipment before studying it closely. "It looks okay Mal," he uttered with a notable sigh of relief. "No visible damage and…" He flicked the on/off switch to on and the camera screen burst into life once again. "Yep, it's fine mate. No drama."

"Well. Just be careful in future, yeah? I don't wanna have to tell my old man that I've managed to fuck his video camera up. Explaining why I had it in the first place would be difficult enough!"

"What?" Wing Nut asked, frowning. "He doesn't even know you've borrowed it?"

"Are you havin' a laugh mate? What would I tell him it's for? Shooting a fuckin' wedding video?"

Wing Nut frowned. "Who do you know that's getting married? I thought everyone you knew was in this room."

Mally opened his mouth to speak but just stood there gaping at his friend in disbelief. Instead of saying something that might complicate matters even further, Mally just shook his head and sighed.

"What?" Wing Nut said. "I'm just sayin' that your dad ain't stupid enough to fall for that line man."

"No Wing Nut," Mally agreed with a sardonic tone. "My dad ain't stupid."

"When you two ladies have finished," Danny interjected. "Can we get started, yeah? I don't like the fuckin' smell in this place." He immediately turned towards Mehmet. "No offence Ghandi," he said with intentional offence.

Mehmet looked at him with utter contempt. "Ghandi was Indian, you thick, uneducated tosser!" He didn't regret the sentiment but he did regret saying it out loud. He just couldn't help himself.

Danny started to advance towards Mehmet, fists tightly clenched. "What the fuck did you say, you little twat?"

Aaron quickly reached out and took a firm grip of Danny's arm, spinning him off track. "What the fuck?" Danny spat angrily, glancing down at his arm in wonder who would actually dare try and stop him. When he saw that it was Aaron - and had registered the look on Aaron's face - his whole demeanour changed to near-sycophantic proportions. "Aw, I was only havin' a laugh Aaron mate," he said nervously. "I wasn't gonna do anything to him, not really. You know me mate? Just pissin' about ha-ha."

"This isn't the time for pissin' about Danny," Aaron growled. "This is the time for showing those bastards out there that we ain't standin' for no more of their Muslim *them-n-us*, *infidel* shit. This is the time to hit them where it hurts; by ridiculing one of their own in front of thousands of YouTube viewers."

"Fuckin' dead right!" Danny shouted with a clap of his hands.

Mally and Wing Nut glanced quickly at each other and frowned; a non-verbal exchange that didn't go unnoticed by Aaron.

117

"Problem boys?" He asked, turning his large body mass intimidatingly towards them. Wing Nut merely shrugged and looked at the floor whilst Mally remained silent. When no answer materialised, Aaron nodded. "Good," he continued and turned towards OD. "Let's get this show…"

"Actually," Mally suddenly said, much to the dismay of his brother.

Aaron frowned and turned back to Mally. "Well?" he asked impatiently. "What's on your mind little man?"

Mally took a deep breath. "We … we're not gonna … you know?" He gestured with his head towards Mehmet.

"We're not gonna what?" Aaron asked.

"You know?" Mally continued. "Kill him or whatever?"

"Fuck me Mally." OD cut in. "What you chattin' bro?"

Aaron held up his hand to silence OD but continued to stare intently at Mally for what seemed like an age. A faint smile suddenly appeared on the big man's face but it was gone in an instant, as though it was an expression he didn't intend to show. "Answer me this little man," Aaron started. "Why have you come here today? In fact," he broke off and glanced at the others standing in the room. "Why did any of you come here today?"

"I didn't have a choice." Mehmet answered, matter-of-factly.

"Shut it nob 'ed." Danny spat. "He wasn't asking you. But, I'll tell you what I'm here for, *Muslim*. To wipe that nasty fuckin' smirk off your greasy face!"

"Well at least you're not calling me a Paki anymore, so we've made some progress."

Danny's face became red and contorted with anger. "Aargh. Fuck. I swear down!" he shouted, turning quickly to Aaron. "Can we just get started now before I really lose it? We all know why we're here, even the gay boy over there." He pointed casually towards Mally.

"Piss off Danny!" Mally retorted.

"Or what rent boy? What you gonna do?" Mally glanced over at his brother, looking for some moral support. "What?" Danny went on with a snort. "You think OD is gonna step in and save his little sister?"

"Leave it now Danny," OD warned. "He's just a bit worried, that's all."

"Fuck *leave it* OD." Danny went on. "Your brother's a shithouse man. If he doesn't want to be here, he should fuck off home to mummy!"

"Nobody is leaving." Aaron said, firmly. "Not until the job is done and we have what we need."

"And what exactly is that?" Wing Nut suddenly piped up. "Because I really have no fuckin' idea what we are doing here today. I thought we were going to spray-paint a few insults on the mosques but now, we've got some innocent lad tied to a chair and a fuckin' video camera set up!"

"Innocent?" Aaron snapped. "You actually believe that this is innocent?" He slapped his hand firmly on to Mehmet's shoulder as though he was a prize animal. "Let's get something straight gentlemen," he continued. "There are two people in this room whose sisters were supposed to go to a concert on May 22nd. One of those sisters suddenly contracted some mysterious illness and - oh dear,

119

couldn't make it - whilst the other..." He broke off and looked directly at Mehmet. Nobody in the room said a word. "Well, we all know what happened to the other sister, don't we pal?" He prolonged his stare at Mehmet with menacing silence and now, nobody in room *dared* to say a word. "You talk about innocence little man?" He called back over his shoulder to Mally. "Then answer me this. Was my sister innocent or did she deserve to die at the hands of these fuckers?" He turned and scanned the other people in the room. "Can *anybody* answer me that question?" Danny wanted to speak but instinctively knew that Aaron hadn't actually finished his *pep* talk. "And what about Abby, my niece? Is she not an innocent child? So why was she condemned to a lifetime of suffering? I'll tell you why. It's because tossers like our friend Mehmet here, think that we are all beneath them and guilty of not following their fucked-up sense of morality. It's because he ..." he pointed directly towards Mehmet without looking at him, like a vehement prosecution barrister might point out the accused to a lethargic jury during his closing argument. "...and all his fuckin' kind want to dominate the world with their crap. I saw it during my tours of duty and I'm still seeing it now, IN MY OWN FUCKING COUNTRY!"

It wasn't so much the change in Aaron's tone that made everyone jump, it was the sudden, yet totally unexpected roundhouse kick that he performed, slamming his foot heavily into Mehmet's torso. Mehmet let out a heavily winded groan as the chair he was strapped to, rocked sideward on two legs and back again. Danny began to bounce up and down on the balls of his feet like an excited child at

Christmas, clapping his hands with giddy impatience whilst cackling like a hyena.

"Yes Aaron!" He cried out with evil glee. "That's what I'm talking about bro'." He quickly stepped forward and swung a hard right into Mehmet's face with a sickening thud. "Fuckin' greasy, Paki cunt!"

Nobody was left in any doubt that either Mehmet's jaw or cheekbone had just been broken, given the subsequent rally of pained yelps.

"Get that thing started!" Aaron barked, pointing loosely towards the video camera whilst glaring at Mehmet. "This little piggy is going to market!"

***

Twenty-Two

"Doesn't look like anyone is home boss." DC Jackson said; his face pressed against the window with his hands cupped around his face to dowse the reflective glare of the glass. "But the light is on in there."

DI Williams sighed before vigorously knocking on the front door once again. "Oh, somebody will be in there all right Jacko. They just don't want to speak to the cops."

"Who does round here?" Jacko muttered, re-joining his boss on the doorstep. He squatted down so that he was at eye-level with the letterbox and lifted the worn metallic flap covering the opening. From this position he could see into the hallway, halfway up the staircase and partially into a room to the left of the front door. It was in that particular room that his eyes settled on something odd, the dim light making it difficult to recognise at first. He squinted slightly, allowing his pupils to adapt and focus on what he was staring at.

And then, he *saw* it.

*

Earlier.

"I don't know what it is you want from me Mister Yilmaz?" Alan said, as he followed the unwelcome visitors into the lounge. "But what I don't want from you, is any sympathy or you telling

122

me that you know how I feel. You don't and I would be…"

Kasim quickly turned around to face Alan and held up his hand, cutting him off mid-sentence. Alan didn't know which was worse: the action itself - ignorant to say the least - or the expression on the man's face. Was that a faint smile? Alan frowned. Kasim spoke.

"As you wish Mister Roberts," he replied. "But what I need from you, is any information that you might have - no matter how insignificant you think it is - regarding the whereabouts of my son."

"I've already told …"

"I know what you said," Kasim interrupted again. "But I would like you to rethink the situation less hastily. My son is missing Mister Roberts and I believe that he will come to some harm if I - we - do not find him soon. So I ask you again, father-to-father, is there anything you can think of? Maybe Kyle has mentioned something to you? After all, he and Mehmet are best friends. Is the boy here? Because I will need to speak to him too."

Alan's patience - thin by nature - disintegrated almost completely as Yilmaz appeared to be *telling* him what he needed, not asking; and nobody - but nobody - told Alan Roberts what to do.

"I don't know how many times I have to tell you before it sinks into that sponge you call a brain." Alan seethed. "But what part of, *I don't know anything about your precious son's whereabouts*, do you not understand?"

Kasim shook his head with disappointment and sighed. "Such a shame Mister Roberts," he said almost apologetically. "Because I believe you do!" Kasim looked at his companion and nodded.

123

Youssef suddenly shot forward with unexpected speed and stealth, gripping Alan by the throat and pushing him back against the wall before Alan even realised he was moving towards him. The movement was on par with a bullfrog uncurling its tongue to snare a fly: quick and precise.

Abby - who had been listening intently and wanted to help Mr Yilmaz in his quest - suddenly understood the phrase about blood being thicker than water and whatever information she was about to impart with him, immediately took a back seat. She might not have a close relationship with her dad but it was *her* dad and nobody laid a finger on him without just cause.

"GET OFF HIM!" she screamed, instinctively getting up out of her wheelchair. The sudden movement caused her to feel light-headed and though she tried to steady herself on the arm of the wheelchair, the shift in weight caused it to fall onto its side. Supported only by weak and painful legs, Abby helplessly staggered forwards. Kasim held out his arm in an attempt to catch the unstable girl but she was just beyond his reach. Abby fell to the floor, catching her head on the corner of the TV unit before coming to rest, facedown.

"Oh my poor child!" Kasim gasped, quickly kneeling down at her side. "Are you alright?"

There was no response. Kasim turned Abby over and saw a deep gash on her forehead that was bleeding profusely and had already left a small pool of dark red on the laminate flooring.

Youssef looked down at the girl and momentarily loosened his grip around Alan's throat, just enough for Alan to struggle free, push Youssef to one side and drop down by his daughter's side.

124

"What the fuck have you done?" He cursed, holding his daughter's head in his hands. "Abby! Abby!"

"By the time I saw her, it was too late." Kasim replied. "I tried to catch her but…"

"Tried my arse." Alan snapped. "This would never have happened if you hadn't shown up here with that fuckin' gorilla over there!"

Kasim leant forward and reached for Abby's hand.

"Get the fuck off her." Alan growled.

"She needs to go to the hospital." Kasim responded.

"Don't you think I know that dickhead? Why don't you call an ambulance instead of stating the obvious?"

Kasim shook his head. "No." he replied succinctly. "They will take too long to get here. We should take her in my car."

"What?" Alan gasped, incredulously.

"Please Mister Roberts?" Kasim pleaded. "It will be a lot faster and I think…" He looked down at Abby, her face now paler than usual. "The sooner we get her there the better."

After a moment's thought, Alan reluctantly agreed. Kasim nodded once again to Youssef who stepped forward and effortlessly gathered up Abby's limp frame in his arms. Within a few minutes, Kasim was driving towards the hospital.

Moments later, a blue coloured Vauxhall Astra - with two occupants on board - passed by on the opposite side of the road. That car was heading for the Roberts' home.

*

"That doesn't look good." DC Jackson remarked, still looking into the house via the letterbox.

"What doesn't?" DI Williams asked.

"There's a wheelchair on its side in there and unless I'm mistaken, that looks like blood on the laminate floor?" Jackson stood up and stepped back to allow his boss to take a look.

"Well, if it's not," Williams said, once he too had peered through the letterbox. "We suspect it could be and that DC Jackson…" He added as he stood back up. "Is our power of entry under section seventeen of PACE, yes?"

"Yes boss," DC Jackson replied with a smile, leant back slightly and raised his foot.

"Er, what you doing Jacko?" Williams asked.

"Well I was about to kick the door in boss."

"For fuck's sake Jacko," Williams sighed. "Have you forgotten the first rule of how not to break your bleeding ankle?" He shook his head slightly in dismay, stepped forward and tried the door handle; this being the first rule. The door immediately swung open and DI Williams knew that he didn't need to say anymore: DC Jackson would already know what a prat he had been.

The detectives stood by the open door of what they presumed, was the lounge area and took in the scene. To the right, a wheelchair lay overturned whilst directly in front of them, there was indeed a small pool of blood on the floor with additional droplets leading to where they were now stood and to the front door. To the left of the room, a reproduced canvas print lay haphazardly on the floor, clearly fallen from the picture hook above on the corresponding wall. The circumstances of what might

126

have occurred, ranged from an innocent explanation to a possible serious assault, or worse. Being cops, neither man present went for the *innocent explanation* option.

"I'll check upstairs boss." Jackson said.

Williams nodded. "Okay. I'll take a look around down here."

Williams went into the kitchen and raised his eyebrows. The work surfaces were laden with dirty dishes and discarded food packets whilst empty beer cans and a couple of newspapers dominated the top of the small kitchen table. He glanced down at the papers and saw a grease stained notepad nestled in amongst the pages of one of them. On it, somebody had written what appeared to be horseracing tips, a few other doodles and…

DC Jackson reappeared from upstairs, joining Williams in the kitchen. "Nothing upstairs boss," he remarked.

Williams grunted slightly but remained staring down at the notepad on the table, flicking a few pages back and forth. "What do you make of this Jacko?" He asked.

DC Jackson walked over, looked down at the pad and frowned. "Looks like somebody has an obsession with whatever or wherever that is, I'd say boss. Why?"

Williams looked up at his Detective Constable. "Get uniform patrols over here to preserve the scene Jacko and ask them to phone the hospitals to see if any of the Roberts' family have been admitted today?"

"Will do." DC Jackson pulled out his mobile phone.

"And when they get here." Williams went on. "You and I are going on another little trip."

"Where to this time boss?" Jackson asked, placing the phone against his ear.

Williams turned his head and gestured towards the notepad. "Angel Court of course!"

***

Twenty-Three

Never did Alan Roberts imagine that he would be sitting in this same position again. Had life not been cruel enough to him already? Or would it simply not be content until all he ever loved - all he ever had - had been taken from him? And was it some fucked-up sense of irony that the same doctor, who had given him the *good news/bad news* story the last time he was here, was now approaching him once again? Alan shot up out of his seat, far from being prepared for the worst but expecting it nonetheless.

*

5th March 2003

Alan paced the corridor outside the operating theatre wishing that the *no smoking* ban would be permanently lifted; or at least until it was all over. He had wanted to be by Angela's side, holding her hand and being called every name under the sun - as he had been during the birth of his two sons - but the procedure currently taking place, was strictly for an audience of medical staff only. Angela's third pregnancy hadn't been an easy time for her and now - having been found by Alan, curled up on the living room floor in extreme pain - she was going through a Caesarean birth, six weeks before the baby was actually due to enter the world.

Alan had been told to prepare for the worst as the baby was in great distress - hence they needed to operate - and given *its* premature state, it's possible *it* might not survive.

"She." Alan remarked, curtly.

"Sorry?" The consultant quizzed.

"The baby is a *she* not an *it*!"

The consultant reddened a little. "Yes, yes of course," he said. "Have you thought of a name for her yet?" He grimaced slightly at his own question. He was just about to deliver a baby that probably wouldn't survive the trauma and here he was making ridiculous pleasantries merely to mask his own ineptitude. Thankfully, he thought, the man before him seemed way too ignorant to notice and - let's be honest - was more likely wondering when he might get back to the pub.

Oh, shame on you Mister Bannister.

"Abigail," Alan replied.

"That's nice." Bannister commented.

"Angela's grandmother's name. They were very close."

"What a nice gesture." Bannister said, with as much sincerity as his disinterested mind could muster. "And I promise," he went on. "That I will do my utmost to honour the memory of her."

"Thank you."

"I will return as soon as I have some news for you Mister Roberts, though I fear that you may be in for rather a long wait."

Alan nodded as the consultant produced some semblance of a reassuring smile, turned on his heels and disappeared through the swing doors of the theatre entrance. Beyond those doors, Alan thought, his wife and yet to be born daughter's fate lay in the hands of God … and some obnoxious ponce who was probably more concerned with when he might get to play his next round of golf.

Oh, shame on you Mr Roberts.

*

At 10:30pm, Abigail Patricia Roberts came into the world weighing four pounds and six ounces and spent the first five weeks of her life in the Special Care Unit at Manchester Royal Infirmary. The consultant in charge gave Abigail a sixty to sixty-five per cent chance of survival following her birth whereas mother and father, on the other hand, were in no doubt about the fate of their daughter.

Bannister was the first to admit his utter amazement over how hard the frail little girl had fought and subsequently pulled through her ordeal.

"Her progress is quite remarkable," he had said in earnest.

"Well, if there's one thing that can be said about our family Mister Bannister," Angela said with beaming pride. "It's that we're a stubborn bunch of fighters and Abigail's shown that she's definitely a *Roberts*."

*

For the next twelve years of her life, Abby was very much the daddy's girl. She was by Alan's side every minute of the day - forever marvelling at his humour, stories and made-up games - and was always the parent she would snuggle up to when the family sat down to watch TV. In short, she adored her dad and he adored her.

"I'm sure you two are joined at the bloody hip." Angela had joked on many occasions. In silent truth, she was a little jealous of the bond they had, a bond that wasn't shaken even when their fourth child was born. Alan showed tremendous fatherly love towards their youngest son, of that there was no doubt, but when it came to his favourite, there was simply no competition for his deepest affection. Then one day - completely out of the blue - that strong father/daughter relationship fizzled out faster than a cheap Chinese firework in a torrential downpour.

"What's up Peanut?" Alan had said to her one morning: a nickname that had derived from a time when, at four years old, Abby had somehow gotten a dry-roasted KP stuck firmly up her nostril.

"You calling me Peanut, for one thing," Abby snapped, uncharacteristically.

"Well, excuse me m'lady," Alan teased, despite being slightly taken aback. "But it's my pet name for you."

"Well, I'm almost thirteen now dad, so can we stick to my *actual* name?"

Alan frowned.

"Where's mum anyway?" Abby quickly added.

"Erm, downstairs. Why?"

"Can you tell her I need her please? And can you close my bedroom door?"

Alan paused for a moment before quietly stepping out of the room and pulling the door to. In truth, he felt a little hurt because up until now, he had always assumed that Abby would only ever *need* him. Stupid, yes, because he also knew that when girls eventually transcend into young women, then all they truly need is the experience and guidance of a mother. Still, even knowing that didn't help.

"Oh she'll come round." Angela had said in an attempt to comfort her forlorn husband. "She's just growing up so fast."

"Hmm. I suppose so." Alan sighed.

"And," she chuckled. "I can't really see you having a heart-to-heart with Abby about her first period, can you?"

Alan managed a smile but still couldn't help feeling rejected. After all, he hadn't even been given the chance to have that *heart-to-heart* with his daughter. And who knows, maybe he would have been a …

Bollocks. His mind quickly interjected. *Who are you trying to kid?*

Alan sighed again, hoping that Angela was right and that Abby would indeed *come around*. He'd just have to wait and see. Not easy for an impatient man.

Over the months that followed, Abby didn't *come around* nor did the strong relationship between father and daughter rekindle. This was due to the fact that Abby - at fourteen years of age - was still very much attached to the hip of her mum, hanging on every word and piece of advice she gave … right up until her mum's premature death.

*

In a constant state of guilt-marred retrospect, Alan was ashamed that he once - if only briefly - hoped that his wife's death would bring him and Abby closer together again. He also thought that - given her injuries - Abby would need him now, more than ever. He couldn't have been more wrong.

If there's one thing that can be said about our family, Alan remembered Angela telling a doctor, *it's that we're a stubborn bunch of fighters. Abigail's definitely a Roberts.*

*

The doctor now heading towards him had the same unreadable expression on his face as he did on the morning of May 23rd … Alan braced himself.

"Hello again Mister Roberts."

Alan was mildly impressed that the doctor remembered his name but there again, why wouldn't he? Their last encounter wasn't exactly an eon ago.

"Is she okay?" Alan asked, bypassing any formalities.

"She's absolutely fine," the doctor replied with a faint smile that Alan presumed was as good a smile as it gets.

Praise Allah, Alan heard Kasim say and for once in his life, he was inclined to agree. *Praise Allah, praise God, praise whoever it was that looked out for my little girl,* he thought, blowing out a long suspire of relief. "Thank you doctor," his voice cracking with emotion. "Thank you so much."

"We will need to keep her under observation for a few more hours," the doctor added. "But that's just a precaution, perfectly normal for anybody who has been rendered unconscious from a head injury."

"Can I see her?"

"Of course you can, although she may be a little drowsy from the painkillers we have given her."

"Thank you."

"And can I just say," the doctor said. "Her recovery from the last time I saw her is, quite

134

frankly, extraordinary. She is clearly a determined young lady."

"She takes after her mum for that," Alan said with fondness.

"However," the doctor continued. "I don't want to see her in A&E again, okay?"

Alan smiled. "Agreed."

"You clearly have a special daughter in Abby, Mister Roberts. Look after her."

"Yes, yes, I will doctor."

As Alan began to walk away with the doctor, Kasim called out to him.

"I will be leaving now Mister Roberts," he said. Alan stopped and turned to face him. "I am truly pleased that Abby will be okay," he went on. "After all, our children are our lives, yes?"

Alan frowned slightly, remaining silent as though he was considering what to say in response. He then walked back over to Kasim.

"Angel Court. Miles platting," he said.

"I'm sorry?"

"Kyle has gone to Angel Court."

"I'm not sure I …"

"He thinks that's where Mehmet might be."

Kasim glared at Alan with an expression that screamed: *Why didn't you tell me this before?* As if fighting to quell an understandable angry response, Kasim merely nodded and walked quickly away.

Yes. Alan thought remorsefully, as he watched him walk away. *Our children* ARE *our lives.*

***

Twenty-Four

June 2005. Afghanistan.

His hearing was the first of his senses to drift back as it registered a sustained, high-pitched note ringing fiercely in his ears; a deep, reactive groan took second place in the list of senses.

As he began to lift his eyelids, the intense bright light of the room that he was in quickly launched an assault on his retinas, causing him to screw his eyes back up again. This in turn made the ringing in his ears seem louder, which resulted in his head pounding like a jackhammer.

He tried to assess the situation, confused at where he was or what was happening. He didn't like not being in control, and he was definitely not in control at the minute. Added to that, it felt as though somebody had just placed a hand across his face, purposely smothering his mouth and nose. He reacted quickly, instinctively beginning to claw at whatever it was that was that was restricting his breathing as he remembered the motto embedded in his mind: *fight or die fighting.*

"Whoa, easy big fella."

The voice was as unrecognisable as it was strangely calming and when cool hands suddenly took a hold of his wrists and moved his arms down to his sides, he offered little resistance.

"It's only oxygen." The voice added with equal tranquillity.

The man cautiously opened his eyes again and scanned his surroundings. He had already gathered that he was on a bed and it looked like he was on some kind of hospital ward but … was he in a tent? He eventually focused on the source of the unfamiliar voice and frowned. A young man, no more than twenty-five years old, was checking a drip, humming a song and writing stuff on a clipboard. He had a stethoscope hanging from his neck and whilst he may have been a doctor, he certainly wasn't dressed like one. Green t-shirt - with an armband displaying a red cross around one of the sleeves - and camouflaged desert combat trousers. It was a surreal setting for the patient, right up until the point when the doctor turned to him, smiled and spoke with that same, unwavering tone of compassion.

"Welcome back Sergeant Berry."

And then - like that post-hypnotic statement - Aaron was immediately, *back in the room.*

"How long have I been out?" He asked, almost matter-of-factly.

"A couple of days," the medic replied, leaning over him to shine a light into his eyes. "Do you remember what happened?"

Aaron would have loved to say *no* but his memory wouldn't fail him on that score: not then, not ever.

*

Two days earlier.

"I hate this fucking heat!" The soldier exclaimed, removing his helmet and rubbing his head vigorously "And if I get bitten by some bored, cunt of a mosquito one more time, I'm gonna shoot some fucker!"

"Stop whinging Corporal," Aaron teased from the adjacent rear seat of the armoured vehicle. "You've got leave coming up in a couple of days haven't you?"

"Can't come soon enough for me Sergeant B," the soldier replied. "Ten days of British weather to look forward to. Never thought I'd miss the rain so fucking much!"

"Piss off Teflon," Aaron joked. "You'll be bored shitless and you know it."

*

Corporal Stuart Campbell was an assertive soldier who - during his career - had found himself the subject of numerous disciplinary hearings; hearings that had been conducted based purely on the malicious complaints of the countrymen whom he had been sent to protect.

Fortunately for Corporal Campbell, his actions were always deemed to have been, *carried out in accordance with military procedure* and none of the allegations had stuck. Thus, the Corporal had acquired his nickname. After all, nothing sticks to Teflon either.

Whilst in Afghanistan, he managed to set himself a new record by being *spoken to* no fewer than six times in three months by his Commanding Officer. Irony, he thought, didn't come close to describing the fact that onlookers had reported him for being *too rough* with the individuals he had stopped and searched on the streets of Marjah in the Helmand Province. Too rough? For fuck's sake.

These were the early, yet fierce, times of Taliban resurgence and there was no Afghani individual - man, woman or child - who wasn't capable of killing a British soldier. Nobody should be beyond suspicion of possessing that capability, so … with the greatest of respect Sir … forgive me for wanting to protect my arse.

Given that the British armed forces were now dealing with a completely different type of evil, he was always granted absolution for his mishaps, without the need to amend his personnel file. The CO was good like that.

*

Teflon and Aaron had become close friends, both joining the armed forces at the same time and both attached to the same regiment from day one. When Aaron got his first promotion, Teflon asked him how many top-brass arses he'd had to kiss to get that undeserved step up the ladder.

"It was a choice between me and some angry, gay, black dude apparently." Aaron replied. "But I guess they're not ready to embrace your womanly ways yet Private Campbell!"

"Listen, Corporal Cunt. I'm more man than you'll ever be and more woman than you'll ever get." Teflon laughed. "And why the fuck would I wanna be a Corp? You'd never see me becoming some arsy Sergeant's bitch!"

Both men had joked about military rank structure yet less than a year later Aaron had been promoted to Sergeant whilst Teflon - with a strong recommendation from Aaron - had been promoted to

Corporal ... and subsequently became the Sergeant's *bitch.*

In reality - embedded beneath the banter - both men had a huge respect for each other and a love that can only be forged between men willing to give their lives for each other. Yes, their *bromance* was joked about by the soldiers that they led but if you asked any one of those soldiers, they would immediately affirm that Sergeant Berry and Corporal Campbell were the best supervision that a unit could have.

*

The date was Tuesday 14th June 2005 when Sergeant Berry was directed to lead a patrol into an area of Marjah that - up until now - had been classed as a safe area. According to his CO, new intelligence suggested that a group of insurgents had taken over two family homes and were storing a sizeable cache of arms under the floor.

"How credible is the intel sir?" Aaron asked.

"Well, Bez," the CO replied. "Given that one of the family members is currently sitting in our holding area, shaking like a shitting dog, I'm reckoning it's pretty credible."

"He came to us?"

"She," The CO corrected. "But yes. She presented herself at the gate in the early hours of this morning. Seems that Grandma isn't too happy about her home being used as ... how did she put it ... *matjar alshaytan?*"

Aaron frowned. "Satan's shop." Two of the twenty-odd Arabic words that he actually knew. "Any possibility it could be a trap?"

140

"Every possibility," the CO replied. "Which is why I need you all to exercise extreme caution with this one lads and lasses, especially given that the homes are conveniently located at the top of a dead end street."

"Fuck me," Teflon sighed. "Is there any good news Sir?"

"Yes Corporal Campbell," the Commanding Officer replied, placing a hand on Teflon's shoulder. "I haven't had a complaint about you in the past week!"

There was rapturous laughter throughout the room.

"Ha-ha," Teflon responded. "Very funny that boss. You should be a comedian!"

The CO smiled and gently squeezed his soldier's shoulder before stepping back into presentation position.

"Seriously though people," he continued, once the laughter had subsided. "We need to watch our backs out there today. No chances, no heroics, let's just keep it simple, do our jobs and return safely, yes?"

"Sir!"

"Bez, Teflon, Mickey, Latino," he added. "You're with me in the lead vehicle. Danny, Pete, Sarah and Carrot, with Sergeant Millington in vehicle two. The rest of you pile into the remaining vehicles. Questions?" He looked around the room but nobody spoke. "Okay. We leave at 0600hrs. Now go get yourselves some breakfast. Dismissed!"

*

"Over there, Mickey." The CO instructed, leaning forward and pointing through the grill-covered windscreen.

The driver pulled across the deserted road and stopped just short of its junction with a narrow side street; the six cylinders, turbocharged diesel engine of the Tempest *MPV* purring like a lion as it idled. Behind them, a further four MPVs pulled up, the occupants ready and waiting for further instructions.

"Right, that's the street there," the CO began. "Too narrow to get the MPVs up there, so we're on foot from here."

"How far up to the target houses boss?" Aaron asked.

"Five, six-hundred meters maybe but, other than the doorways of the houses leading up there, there is very little cover between the rooftops and the street."

"So we're looking at a dynamic deployment?"

"Exactly," the CO confirmed whilst pulling out a map of the area. "The target houses, here and here," he continued, pointing on the map. "Are connected to the backs of houses on the next street, here and here."

"So, only one way in and one way out." Teflon commented.

"Well," The CO replied. "Unless they have knocked through the back walls to use as an escape route, which is highly possible. So, I need the teams in vehicles three and four to deploy up this next street here - whatever it's fucking called - and cover the houses backing on to our targets. The team in the last vehicle are to remain here as back-up."

"Roger that boss." Aaron said. "I'll go and brief the others."

He opened the vehicle door and stepped out onto the road.

*

It had only been three months since Ahmed Omar - the seventeen-year-old son of a baker - pledged his allegiance to the Taliban and became a *Mujahidin,* but he was already beginning to have serious doubts about their interpretation and enforcement of *Sharia*: Islamic Law.

As naïve as it was, he had truly believed that he would be fighting to restore peace and stability amongst his fellow Afghans, who were constantly being manipulated by the false claims and ungodly acts of the western societies. But, he had joined the Taliban with his eyes wide shut and his head filled with ideologies of a better future and by the time he had learned the true reality of their violent methods, he was in way too deep to get out. There was another factor why he couldn't leave of course - a factor that was way more influential than the threat of becoming an outcast: pride. His father - a humble yet intelligent man - had seen Ahmed's attitude change since he had started college and, sadly, it wasn't for the better. He feared the path that his son might take and had warned, advised and done everything within his power to stop Ahmed making the wrong choice; making a bad choice. Ahmed had resisted, argued with, and eventually defied his father, calling him a traitor to his own country before storming out of the house. Now though, three months on, he wished he had listened to his father. He dearly wanted to return to the family home and beg forgiveness, if only his pride would let him. As it was, he was now stuck on a roof keeping a look out for military infidels, in a section of Marjah that hadn't been patrolled by western armed forces in weeks. Not only that, but the houses in which the Taliban were storing weapons were so *normal*, that nobody would be interested in approaching them let alone searching them.

It had been a long night and - just like the night before - nothing had happened: unless you count seeing some woman scurrying along the street below at 2am. Unusual behaviour perhaps but not suspicious enough to report, especially as the woman in question appeared to be as old as his grandmother.

He sighed, reached into his pocket and pulled out a battered packet containing four cigarettes. The cigarettes had been in there since the day he found the discarded packet over two months ago but that's because he didn't actually smoke. The Taliban forbid its fighters from carrying anything on their person that might identify them if captured by the enemy … photos, ID cards, letters and so-forth … but Ahmed didn't quite grasp the point. Despite that, he wasn't stupid enough to let himself be caught with something that he shouldn't have, so, he had modified the cigarette packet he'd found by constructing a small, secret compartment within it. Hence, the four cigarettes remained untouched. In that compartment he had hidden a photograph; a photograph that he had now removed and unfolded. He sat down with his back against the wall and smiled lovingly at the image in his hands. His mother, father, sisters and baby brother smiled back.

It was 4am on Tuesday 14th June 2005 when he allowed his eyes to close … just for a little while.

*

At 6.30am, Ahmed was jolted from his sleep by a low rumble of thunder. He looked up at the sky and frowned at the unexpected appearance of it: clear and blue with the sun already hitting the rooftops. In his half-asleep-half-awake state, he still thought that he could hear thunder somewhere in the distance but then - like a splash of ice-cold water in the face - he realised exactly what it was that he was listening to.

"Shit!" he exclaimed, as he moved quickly onto his knees. "Please Allah, let me be wrong!"

Once he was in position, he took a deep breath, carefully lifted his head above the parapet of the building and looked down onto the street.

"Oh shit, oh shit!" He immediately crouched back down again. His heart was pounding, his whole body perspiring from both fear and excitement. He needed to take another look. Carefully and precisely, Ahmed raised his head again and assessed the street below. He saw four - no five - British Army vehicles parked next the kerb with their engines still idling. For a while, it didn't look as though anybody was going to get out of the MPVs, so he just continued to observe, assuming that they would eventually move on. But then, one of the doors of the lead vehicle opened up and a soldier stepped out onto the road.

***

Twenty-Five

When you poke a stick into an ant's nest, the ants will quickly and silently egress from their habitat: not in a state of panic but in a state of battle, ready to defend their Queen and fight to the death if necessary. A little after 0630hrs on Tuesday 14th June 2005, that same principal was applied to an area of Marjah in the Helmand Province of Afghanistan, only this time, the stick was the British Army being poked into a nest of Taliban insurgents.

The radio message from Ahmed had been simple but effective, causing the occupants of two particular *nests* to emerge with speed and stealth. They took up their positions on rooftops, in doorways and at windows, ready to fight to the death.

The radio message back to Ahmed had been even simpler, which is why his index finger was now poised to apply pressure to the trigger of his AK47 assault rifle.

*

Sergeant Berry instinctively checked his surroundings as he stepped out of the MPV paying particular attention to the rooftops. He was always wary of being exposed in a built up area; too many nooks and crannies for the enemy to hide in. Satisfied that there appeared to be no immediate threat, he made his way to the other vehicles and briefed his colleagues on the CO's plan of action.

146

The soldiers alighted from the cover of their respective Tempests - also with speed and stealth - and advanced towards their target. As they rounded the street on which the suspect houses were located, Aaron held up his hand as a signal to stop and hold. He then waited for confirmation - two clicks on the encoded radio - that a team was in position on the adjacent street. The green light came, Aaron gestured once more and the unit moved forward.

*

Ahmed peered down the sights of his rifle, watching the soldiers as they advanced into the street below him and then stopped. His heart was pounding like a big bass drum in his chest; was this his moment?

During his time as a Taliban fighter, he had never actually fired a single shot against the enemy but that was because he had never been used as anything other than a messenger boy. Now though, it looked like this would be his time to shine and finally get to do what he'd been trained to do. He was focused, he was excited and he was thankful: thankful that he hadn't eaten a great amount recently because he was also extremely nervous. After all, it was a big deal to kill a man in cold blood for the first time, whether it was Allah's will or not. But he was ready and it was time.

"Allahu Akbar!" He shouted, as he quickly jumped up and began to fire indiscriminately at the soldiers below him. That's when all hell broke loose.

*

"Hostiles! Take cover!" Aaron shouted as some twenty-plus insurgents suddenly appeared on the surrounding rooftops and opened fire. Thankfully for Sergeant Berry and his team, Ahmed had proved to be a useless shot and his lethal bullets had merely hit and embedded themselves in the walls of the houses. Unluckily for Ahmed, a British soldier with way more experience and a much better aim, had returned fire. Ahmed Omar - the seventeen-year-old son of a baker - was still shouting and still firing, when a single shot to the head ended his life.

*

From somewhere at the back of him, a soldier shouted *RPG*, meaning that an insurgent had been spotted, aiming a rocket-propelled grenade towards them. Aaron looked up, saw the fighter with the weapon on his shoulder and immediately fired a burst of bullets at the threat. The insurgent went down but not before the RPG had been activated. The deadly grenade zipped through the air but went wide of its intended target, causing Aaron to blow out a breath of momentary relief. He glanced to the opposite side of the street and saw Teflon, standing in a doorway giving him the thumbs up and smiling that infectious smile of his. Aaron shook his head, smiled back and watched as Teflon stepped out from the doorway and advanced. The subsequent explosion from the IED that Teflon stepped on, ripped into the building beside it, throwing shrapnel-infused rubble across and down the street. Aaron was thrown backwards by the force, peppered by debris and knocked unconscious as he slammed into the stonewall of a house opposite.

Despite the blackness, despite the ringing in his ears, he could hear his name being called, which meant he was still alive.

"Aaron? … Aaron?"

He heard his name again but it was said by a voice that he didn't recognise. He tried to concentrate on the vocal tone as his name was spoken once again.

And then - as if it was the most obvious thing in the world - it suddenly came to him.

*

"Aaron?" A little louder than the youth had wanted to say it, but he was becoming slightly impatient.

Aaron continued to stare out of the broken window across the dark land below, not moving an inch.

"It's getting late," he eventually said, matter-of-factly.

There was complete silence in the room with everyone confused as to what was actually going on. All eyes were now on Aaron, except for Mehmet's. He was looking towards the door that led out onto the landing; his best friend Kyle was staring back.

***

Twenty-Six

The evening sky had finally given way to night and despite the sound of some unrelenting dog barking in the distance, it was unusually silent.

Though it was a night when the moon was scheduled to be full, its shine had been extinguished by the presence of thick, pitiless cloud. The nearby streetlights - those that worked - did little to break the darkness though it didn't seem to faze one man's objective.

"What are you doing Jacko?" DI Williams asked, when he saw DC Jackson pulling tentatively at a fence panel.

Jackson glanced back at his boss. "Seeing if we can get in through here."

"You got a torch?"

"Not on me."

"Then how the fuck are we going to see where we're stepping?"

"It's not that dark boss." Jackson replied, casually looking up at the sky before realising what a stupid remark it was. "Okay," he quickly conceded. "Maybe it is. But we need to get in there, sooner rather than later."

"And we will." Williams assured him. "Just as soon as a uniformed patrol gets here with a Mag Light. I'm not ruining my shoes for the sake of ten minutes Jacko, they cost more than your shed of a car!"

"Whoa, steady on," the DC cut in. "Don't

dis the car, it's vintage that is. They don't build them like that anymore."

"Thank fuck for that!"

Both men smiled, until they heard the sound of loud banging coming from somewhere just beyond the derelict high-rise.

"What the fuck was that?" Jacko asked.

"Something that negates us waiting for uniform to arrive." Williams stepped forwards. "Grab hold of that fence panel again Jacko!"

*

Only one of the men needed to pull at the fence panel and he did it with such force that only three attempts were needed to rip the rusty metallic panel from its weary posts. As it came away, he threw it to one side as though it were a paper plane and stepped eagerly through the gap.

"Hold on a minute Youssef," Kasim said and reached into his jacket pocket. When he produced a small torch mounted on a key ring and held it out to his cousin, Youssef simply raised his eyebrows. Kasim smiled. "I always carry it with me," he explained. "You never know when it will come in handy."

Youssef shrugged and took the torch from Kasim. When he turned it on, he nodded his silent approval at the intensity of the beam from such a small gadget.

"Not everything that is useful is big, cousin." Kasim gibed with a smile. Youssef grunted, the joke lost on him: or was it? One could never tell with Youssef.

*

From opposite sides of Angel Court, two pairs of men entered the surrounding, overgrown grounds at the same time; both pairs were looking for the same youth but neither expected to find what they did.

*

"What the fuck's going on?"

Everyone in the room turned quickly towards the door, all except for Aaron, who remained staring intently out of the window.

"Fuck me, look who it is." Danny said. "Nice of you to eventually join us mate."

"I'm not your mate Danny." Kyle spat back bitterly and then looked beyond the now-frowning youth. "Aaron?" he called. No response. Kyle shook his head in dismay and turned to Mehmet. "You okay bro?"

"I've felt better," Mehmet replied. "But I'll live." He glanced at Aaron. "I hope."

Kyle stepped towards his bound friend. "OD," he said, looking at the stunned youth. "Help me untie him, yeah?"

OD took one step forward but immediately stopped when Aaron spoke. "Leave him!" he growled. "Our work isn't done!"

"Work?" Kyle questioned, angrily. "What fucking work, Aaron? Don't you think you've done enough to him? This shit needs to end, now!"

"It ends when I say it ends Kyle." Aaron turned towards his nephew. "And not before!"

"Before what exactly?" Kyle asked.

"Before he gets what's coming to him," Danny quickly cut in. "He needs to pay for what his fucking Paki Taliban mate did at the Arena!"

Ignorance personified. Kyle thought.

"You really are a thick fuck, aren't you Steele?" Kyle scoffed.

"Watch your mouth Kyle," Danny retorted. "Chattin' shit to me will get you banged out bro, seriously!"

"Really?" Kyle laughed sarcastically. "By you? Fuck off you muppet. This lot might be scared of your nasty mouth but that's all it is, a nasty mouth. You ain't got the marbles to follow through unless you're with a fuckin' posse!"

Danny clenched his fists and took a step towards Kyle. Kyle took two steps towards Danny and suddenly, they were inches apart.

"And what?" Kyle snarled. "You wanna try your luck, you little rat?

Up until that moment, Danny didn't realise that Kyle had three inches height over him and was noticeably bigger in build and this left Danny with a dilemma. Should he have a go, probably get beaten and lose face or, back down, avoid the battle and … well … lose face? With all eyes watching, Danny did what any self-respecting bully full of false bravado would do: he bullshitted.

"I wouldn't want to embarrass you in front of your uncle, bro," he sneered. "Plus, we've got shit to deal with right now." He glanced at Mehmet. "But," he continued, facing Kyle again. "Once we've done 'ere, I'll be happy to educate you. Pakis, faggots. I don't care, you're all the same to me!"

Kyle lunged forward, grabbed Danny by the throat and pushed him backwards into the wall.

Danny tried to resist but the element of surprise had left him unbalanced and unable to push back.

"Enough!" Aaron shouted, just as Kyle pulled back his arm, ready to throw a punch. Kyle seemed held in a freeze frame, glaring at Danny as though considering his options. Eventually, he dropped his arm and loosened his grip, giving Danny the opportunity to push him away.

"You're a fuckin' dead man walking Roberts!" he spat. "Trust me!"

"I said, enough!" Aaron growled. "Leave your shit for later, we've got…"

The loud bang cut him off mid-sentence. He turned and looked back out of the window again.

"What the fuck was that?" Wing Nut asked.

"I dunno." Mally replied. "But I think we need to fuck off. This is getting too serious."

"I'm with you bro." Wing Nut agreed and turned to Owen. "OD? You coming mate?"

"Yeah," OD replied. "Fuck this shit, let's go."

"Stay where the fuck you are." Aaron said, as he peered through the broken glass. "And turn that fucking light off." Wing Nut turned to his friends and shrugged, wondering what their next move should be. "NOW!" Aaron shouted, making Wing Nut jump and quickly fumble for the video light switch. Darkness consumed the room in an instant and it took a while for all eyes to adjust to the new ambience, all except for Aaron's that is. He was used to environments that changed at the drop of a hat: when you go from the bright, burning sun of an Afghan sky, into the darkness of a suspected insurgent house, you have to be.

Once he had heard the bang, he had quickly scanned the waste ground below them, looking for

154

signs of anything unusual. Something had caught his eye and he focused on the spot where he thought he had seen movement. And then he saw it. Torchlight.

"What is it Aaron?" Danny asked. "What have you seen man?"

Aaron turned away from the window. "We need to take him upstairs," he said, nodding towards Mehmet.

"What?" Kyle interjected. "Nah, fuck that man!"

"I'm bouncing out of here." Wing Nut said. "This has gone way too far already."

"Me too." Mally said.

"Yeah, fuck this bollocks." OD agreed. "Let's go!"

As they started to collect their bags, Aaron casually reached behind his back and pulled out a handgun that he had concealed in his waistband.

"WHOA, WHOA!" Kyle shouted out, holding up his hands and stepping backwards.

Wing Nut, OD and Mally froze whilst Danny simply smiled and whispered: *yes Aaron.*

"I'm not pissing about here ladies." Aaron commanded. "Now take that little cunt upstairs or I swear to god, I will start using this." He cocked the gun and held it out at arms length. "Test me and see if I don't!"

"Aaron, what the hell?" Kyle tried, with a noticeable tremble in his voice.

"Your unc' is serious bro," Danny grinned malignantly. He stepped towards Aaron. "And can I just say…"

Aaron pointed the gun directly at Danny. "Nah, you've said way too much already you little weasel. So, shut the fuck up and let's get moving. We need to

155

finish this." Everybody remained perfectly still, shocked by the sudden escalation, held by overwhelming fear. "NOW!" Aaron shouted, suddenly pressing the gun into Mehmet's temple. "Unless you want me to redecorate this room in a shade of Muslim?"

The group moved quickly towards the communal stairs just beyond the flat's front door. Kyle - watched carefully by Aaron - untied Mehmet and helped him to his feet, holding onto him whilst he regained some stability. From the stench, Kyle knew that his friend had soiled himself but who could blame him? He looked into the tear-filled eyes of Mehmet, sensing his own tears forming. "You'll be okay man," he whispered. "I promise."

Mehmet responded with a faint smile yet knew it was a promise that Kyle might not be able to keep.

Sadly, Kyle knew it too.

***

Twenty-Seven

Youssef stopped in his tracks, turned to Kasim and then nodded his head up towards the first floor of the building.

"You saw it too?" Kasim asked rhetorically. "I thought I was imagining it at first but there was definitely a light coming from that room."

He considered the situation for a moment whilst Youssef remained perfectly still: not unlike a faithful dog waiting for his master's next command.

*

On the other side of the building, DC Jackson also stopped, staring up at the building's stairwell that jutted out from the main structure. Though most of the window panes were opaque - and surprisingly still intact - there were a few on the lower levels that had been smashed, making it possible to see into the stairwell itself … during daylight hours that was. However, at this time of the day, the darkness had swallowed up whatever light there was and created the illusion that black panels had replaced the glass.

"What's up Jacko?" Williams asked.

Jackson shook his head slightly. "I'm not sure. I thought I saw something move up there."

Williams followed his DC's stare up to the side of the building and frowned. "It's pitch black," he said. "How could you see anything?"

Jackson shrugged. "I dunno. Maybe my eyes are playing … wait, look. The next level up!"

"Yeah, I see it. Just." Williams confirmed. "Not very bright but…"

"I'm guessing that somebody's using the torch on their mobile phone to light the way."

"And they're going up." Williams moved forward. "C'mon Jacko," he directed. "We need to get inside before whoever that is, loses themselves in amongst twenty-odd floors of crap!"

*

"I've only got five per cent left on my phone bro." Danny looked back into the gloom of the stairwell towards Aaron. "Maybe we should use that video light?"

"No!" Aaron snapped. "They'll see it."

Kyle turned quickly to glare at his uncle "Who will see it?" He asked suspiciously.

Aaron quickly realised his mistake and did what any other armed and unstable man backed onto on the ropes might do: he pointed his gun at the group and threatened them. "Just keep fucking moving and stop all the chat," he growled. "Or I'm gonna start thinking that you're all pussies who want out. And that ain't happening until we deal with our friend here!"

Mehmet shot Aaron a look of disgust. "Friend?" He said. "If this is how you treat your friends, I'm surprised you still have any!"

Aaron ignored Mehmet and looked directly at Kyle. "You need to keep your little Muslim pal in check nephew, because if he looks at me like that again, I'll shoot him in the fucking face. Comprender?"

"Fucking do it then!" Mehmet called out.

Three of the group gasped whereas only one developed a psychotic smile. The latter hoped that his phone battery would last long enough to illuminate the aftermath of that death wish statement.

Aaron swung the gun around and held it inches away from Mehmet's forehead. "Say that again, you little twat," he whispered. "I dare you!"

"Aaron, no!" Kyle pleaded, quickly placing his hand on top the gun. "He didn't mean it man, he's just … fuck … c'mon man, lower the gun yeah?"

For what seemed like an eternity, Aaron and Mehmet locked eyes with a palpable intensity. It was like the grand final in that world-renowned game of *whoever blinks first, loses,* and neither competitor seemed willing to lose. Whether it was an act of bravado, anger or just plain stupidity, Mehmet moved his head forwards and pressed his skull firmly against the barrel of the gun.

"Go on then," he spat, defiantly. "Do it. You're gonna do it anyway so just get it over with!"

"What the fuck Mehmet?" Kyle gasped. "Shut up bro!"

"Nah," Danny cackled. "Keep diggin' that hole man, this is fucking mint!"

"Shut your trap Danny," OD hissed. "This is fucking insane!"

"You're not kidding." Wing Nut agreed, paused, and then added: "Fuck it. I'm outta here." He started down the stairs, stopped, and then looked back over his shoulder. "You coming Mally? OD?" he asked.

The unexpected retort of the gun was deafening inside the confined space of the stairwell. Somebody screamed, whilst another involuntarily soiled himself.

Mehmet - watched by a horrified Kyle - instantly dropped to the floor.

*

DI Williams and DC Jackson had just entered the stairwell when they heard the gunshot.

"Fuck me!" Jackson called, as he and his boss simultaneously flinched and ducked down.

"Out Jacko, NOW!" Williams commanded, pushing his colleague back through the doorway.

Jackson turned left, looking to exit the building the same way they came in, but Williams held him back.

"Not that way Jacko. We'll be open targets if whoever is up there decides to start popping shots off from the window!"

Jackson nodded and headed in the opposite direction to the building's emergency exit. He only hoped that whatever company had initially secured the building, had secured that door with an equal lack of enthusiasm.

Seconds later he was pushing down on the locking bar of the emergency exit door and silently praying.

He felt some relief as the door swung outwards with surprisingly relative ease, though his heart missed more than a few beats when he almost ran into the mountain of a man standing on the other side of it.

*

"MEHMET!" Kyle shouted as he watched his best friend fall.

With a delayed reaction - a delay that had already convinced Kyle of the worst - Mehmet suddenly let out an agonised scream; the result of a perforated eardrum and cordite scorched skin.

He glared at Aaron. "What did you do that for, you fucking psycho? You could have fucking killed me!"

Aaron smiled unnervingly. "If I wanted you dead," he replied, "you would have been dead!"

Mehmet's mind instantly registered and replayed the words that Aaron had just spoken, and hope sprung eternal.

If I wanted you dead, you would have been dead ... That's what he said, right? IF I wanted you dead. Does that mean he doesn't? Is he just acting out this nightmare to ...?

"But it's not that time yet Muslim boy!" Aaron added, immediately severing Mehmet's mental lifeline. "Now, all of you," he continued, looking at the others, "get fucking moving or trust me, the next bullet won't end up in the wall." He turned to Kyle before adding. "No exceptions, nephew. Get that twat up onto his feet and let's get a shimmy on. There's work to be done." Aaron moved over to the stairwell window and peered through the broken glass, suddenly lost in whatever world he was a part of.

Slowly and nervously, the group began to ascend the stairs as Kyle offered Mehmet a helping hand.

"Piss off Kyle," Mehmet hissed, swatting away Kyle's hand as though it was an irritating Bluebottle. "Uncle-fucking-Aaron there is out of control man and I don't need his poor relation to help me onto my feet, I need him to stop that lunatic!"

Kyle shrugged, his eyes glazing over. "I don't know how to," he replied quietly. "It's like something deep inside him has seriously snapped."

"Really? D'ya think?" Mehmet scoffed. "I hadn't fucking noticed!"

"No … yeah …I know, but this is…"

"What? Nothing personal?"

"I didn't mean it like that but actually, I don't think it is. He's in another zone. Fuck, I don't know!"

"Well," Mehmet slowly rose to his feet. "That makes me feel a whole lot fucking happier now mate. Thanks for the heads-up!" He barged his way past Kyle and headed up the stairs.

"Mehmet? Mehmet?"

"Save it Kyle." Mehmet called back as he disappeared into the darkness.

"Yeah, save it Nephew," Aaron cut in, without looking away from the window.

Kyle turned to Aaron, wondering where the man he knew - and loved - had gone. He opened his mouth to say something but knew whatever he had to say would fall on the deafest of ears.

"Do you reckon my mum would be proud of you now?" There was no reply.

As Kyle walked away, Aaron lowered his head and blinked away an unexpected tear that had formed in his eye. *Maybe his sister wouldn't be proud of him right now,* he thought; *but sometimes we gotta do what we gotta do.* He held up the gun in his hand, checked it over and returned it to the waistband of his jeans. "And this Ang'," he whispered to a woman who wasn't there. "Is something I gotta do."

***

Twenty-Eight

"Jesus!" Jackson startled as he looked up at the man towering before him. "Who the hell are you?"

"We could ask you the same question?" Came a reply from somebody hidden from view behind the initial man's large frame.

In a near-comedic double take, DC Jackson and DI Williams looked at each other, frowned and tilted their bodies sideward to look beyond the man in front of them.

"We're the Police," Williams said, studying the slight man. "And I'm guessing that you're related to Mehmet Yilmaz?"

"I'm his father," Kasim replied.

"Well Mister Yilmaz, I need you and..." He glanced at the big man.

"My cousin, Youssef," Kasim helped.

"You and Youssef here, to move back to the other side of the fence."

"I'm sorry officer," Kasim replied with a surreal calm. "But that won't be possible."

"I beg your pardon?" Williams frowned.

"You heard the gunshot I presume officer?"

"Yes, and that's why I need you..."

"And you realise that my son might be in there?"

"We have no confirmation of that Mister Yilmaz," Williams said, becoming a little vexed. "But we do have confirmation that there is somebody up there with a firearm and as we have no idea who that is or why they would have a firearm, is all the

163

more reason to move back to a safe area and re-assess the situation."

"By which time," Kasim replied. "My son, if he is in there - and I believe, as you do, that he is - could be badly hurt or killed. So, thank you for your concern officer but I won't be moving back whilst you *re-assess* the situation. I need to help my child!"

"I'm sorry Mister Yilmaz," Williams said bluntly. "But I can't allow that to happen!"

"What will you do officer?" Kasim asked sardonically. "Arrest me?"

Williams sighed. "If that's what it takes," he replied. "But I'd rather we didn't go down that route Mister Yilmaz as that doesn't help anyone, let alone your son."

Youssef let out a grunt which Kasim - and only Kasim - interpreted as a sign of agreement.

"Very well," Kasim sighed, after a small pause for thought. "We will do it your way, for now."

"Thank you Mister Yil…"

"But if no significant progress is made within the hour," Kasim quickly added. "Then I *will* be going in there, with or without your permission!"

Williams nodded. "Agreed," he said. "Now can we please just start heading out?"

As Kasim and Youssef turned and began to walk back the way they came, DC Jackson looked at his boss. "One hour? Really?" He whispered. "You'll be lucky to get the firearm boys down here before that boss."

"Yeah, I know that Jacko," Williams replied. "But better to stall for sixty minutes and come up with something, rather than letting Yilmaz and Mohammed The Mountain storm in there, all guns blazin' … pardon the pun."

Inside the shell of Angel Court, seven people had slowly ascended the concrete stairs to the twenty-second floor. Six of them had no idea what the seventh person was planning next, nor why he had instructed them to stop on this particular floor, but nobody was willing to ask the question.

"In there." Aaron pointed to a door that was numbered 220.

The group stole a momentary glance at each other before making their way into the flat; each and every one of them was taken aback once they got inside.

Although it was situated in the same decaying, condemned building, the flat itself - illuminated by several portable lamps - was close to being immaculate, which left nobody in any doubt that Aaron had actually been living there; nobody apart from Danny that is, who was a little slow on the uptake.

"Fuck me," he gasped. "How come this place ain't like the other shit holes? Looks like some cheeky twat has been living here rent-free, if you ask me. Proper little shag pad this is."

"Danny!" OD hissed with a reprimanding tone.

"What?" Danny replied, with a vexed frown.

"Shut the fuck up bro!"

Danny opened his mouth to object but then saw the look on OD's face and his eyes flicking back and forth towards Aaron. Danny's frown eased when the penny finally dropped and his face turned a dark shade of crimson.

"Shit," he said. "Sorry Aaron. I didn't mean that you … well, you're not but, y'know what I…"

"Set the camera up there," Aaron interrupted, saving Danny from digging an even deeper hole for himself. He then gestured towards Mehmet. "And sit him down over there." Aaron pointed to a chair that, up until now, nobody had really registered: standing alone, away from everything else. Nothing unusual about that, but being stood on top of a plastic sheet made it look very sinister, especially as everyone in the room had already second guessed what the sheet might be for.

"Hey." Mally suddenly called. "There's somebody down there with a torch." He moved his head closer to the large window. "Hang on, there's four of 'em and…"

"Get away from the fucking window," Aaron growled.

Kyle stared at his uncle until his uncle caught him doing so.

"What?" Aaron asked, tetchily.

"Is that who you were on about before?" Kyle quizzed.

"What are you talking about?"

"Before, on the stairs. We wanted to use the video light but you said no because, *they'll see us*. Was it them?"

"I don't know what you're chattin' nephew but you're making no sense." He turned back to the group now gathered at the window. "I told you lot to move away from the window and get…" He suddenly broke off, and glanced quickly around the room. "Ah, FUCK!" he shouted, removed the gun from his waistband and headed quickly towards the door.

*

166

At first, Mehmet had frozen, not sure what to do with the opportunity that had just presented itself to him. The majority of the people in the room had gone over to the window when the one they called *Mally* had seemingly spotted somebody outside, whilst Kyle remained engaged in a conversation with his uncle … who had his back turned.

Mehmet knew that he only had seconds in which to act before all eyes were back on him. The door was open, there was nothing in between him and that door - and possible escape - but could he move? His heart pounded whilst his legs felt as though somebody had tied weights around them and then nailed his feet to the floor.

Move, he told himself. *Now*!

He eventually managed to put one leg back and then pull the other along side it.

One step … and nobody had noticed.

He moved again.

Two steps … three, four.

And just like that, he was suddenly standing by the doorway.

He turned and walked forward, waiting for somebody to spot him and raise the alarm but nobody did. Miraculously, he found himself halfway down the hallway with the front door in view. Only a few more steps and he would be out, just a few more and…

Ah FUCK!

Hearing Aaron's loud expletive, Mehmet knew that his absence had now been noticed. He also knew that the distance between him and the front door was far greater than the distance from where he had just come. Running was out of the question - not least because of the pain he felt throughout his body from

167

his ordeal so far - but he couldn't just stand there and do nothing.

Aaron stomped out from the living room whilst Mehmet held his breath and prayed.

*

Aaron pounded down the hallway and out through the front door, hurriedly followed by the majority of the group; Kyle and Mally remained where they were. Danny could be heard casting blame amongst the posse, right up to the point where the front door closed behind them and muffled out the accusatory words.

In the dark stairwell, Aaron closed his eyes and tried to listen but the fools that were with him came barging in, shattering his focus with their fucking bickering.

"QUIET!" He barked. The effect was like muting the tune in a game of musical statues. Nobody moved, nobody spoke; in fact, it was hard to tell if anyone was actually breathing.

Aaron turned his attention to listening again when suddenly - from some floor above - there was the sound of a stairwell door closing to. He immediately began to ascend the stairs, followed by Danny. Wing Nut took a step forward but OD suddenly grabbed his arm and held him back.

"Hang on bro." OD stepped forward and glanced up into the dark stairwell. He listened until the sound of hurried footsteps began to fade away and then turned back to Wing Nut. "Right. This is our chance to piss off man."

"What?" Wing Nut replied, looking confused.

"Look mate, they don't realise we haven't followed them up there yet. And, whilst they go up, we can go down and get the fuck out!" Wing Nut remained silent as if considering the proposition. "It's now or never man." OD added, wondering what was so difficult for his friend to grasp.

Wing Nut eventually nodded his head. "We need to go get Kyle and Mally first," he said.

"Like, now." OD concurred, turning back towards the stairwell door.

*

In the hallway of the flat - located between the front door and the living room - was a small coat cupboard, its door slightly ajar. Peering through the gap from inside, Mehmet watched as Aaron passed and headed out of the front door.

When he had heard Aaron curse moments earlier, he knew that he had three choices: Run - although he was in too much pain for that one - give himself up, or hide. As futile as the last option seemed, it was that choice that had placed him inside this tiny enclosure. Had there been anything inside it, there would have been no chance he could have pulled the door to but thankfully, there was nothing more than cobwebs and a strong smell of cat urine.

Seconds after Aaron had passed, three of the remaining group followed him out, leaving just Kyle and Mally in the flat. Mehmet waited a few moments longer, stepped tentatively out of the closet and walked back into the living room.

"Mehmet!" Kyle acknowledged with genuine surprise. "Where did…"

"I hid in the cupboard," Mehmet replied, anticipating the question.

Kyle walked over to him and did something that nobody would have expected: he hugged his friend. "We need to get you out of here bro and fast, before Aaron works out what's happened!"

"You got that right man," a voice from behind them agreed. Mehmet quickly turned around whilst Kyle looked over his shoulder. OD and Wing Nut appeared at the living room door, much to the relief of all others present. "Aaron and Danny are only a couple of floors up." OD continued. "So we need to get a shift on."

OD, Wing Nut, Kyle, Mally and Mehmet quickly headed for the front door.

Taking hold of the handle, OD paused and then turned towards Mehmet. "I'm sorry about the shit you've been through mate," he said with sincerity. "It was never meant to … well, I'm sorry yeah?"

Mehmet's expression told OD that this wasn't the day he was going to accept an apology and to be fair, why should he?

OD nodded his understanding, turned back and pulled the front door open.

"Well, well, well," Danny said, standing outside the front door. "Going somewhere ladies?"

***

Twenty-Nine

March 2005. Afghanistan.

The notes were soft and tender, as one would expect from a musical ballad, but played by Michael McKenzie, it was almost hypnotic.

Latino - the MPV driver - had pulled up beneath the cover of a balcony on a large building to allow the army personnel inside to disembark and stretch their legs for five minutes. Private McKenzie saw this as an opportunity to pull out his harmonica and play the tune he had been working on.

"Looks like you've got your biggest audience to date over there Mickey." Corporal Campbell nodded towards a small stonewall on the opposite side of the road.

Private McKenzie stopped playing and glanced sideways, chuckling when he saw a lone Afghani boy sitting on the wall, watching on. The boy was no more than twelve years old, clothed in a torn and dirty Adidas t-shirt and football shorts that were clearly made for an adult. His feet were filthy from the lack of shoes but they had seemingly grown accustomed to the harsh mixture of grit and rubble that made up the ground. McKenzie gave him a wave; not a wave to say hello, more like a rock star would give out to his adoring fans as he left the stage. "Thank you," McKenzie shouted. "You've been great!"

The boy smiled an almost toothless grin and waved back. He then made a small series of hand gestures towards McKenzie, a look of hope on his unwashed face.

"What?" McKenzie called back, holding up his harmonica. "You wanna try this little man?"

The boy nodded enthusiastically and jumped down from the wall as Private McKenzie began to head over to him.

"Whoa, careful Mickey," Aaron warned. "Get him to walk to you."

Private McKenzie stopped dead and mentally chastised himself. He knew better than to walk across untested ground towards what could be a Taliban decoy. IEDs (improvised explosive devices) hidden in the dirt, sniper fire, suicide attacks; all very real and present dangers, especially when venturing into open territory. "Fuck. Yeah. Sorry Sarge," he replied and gestured at the boy to come over to him.

The boy hesitated at first, looked around and then walked quickly over to McKenzie, presenting that same near toothless grin when he arrived.

"What's your name kiddo?" McKenzie asked, returning a smile.

"I am Akbar Mohammed Kamal, sir," the boy proudly replied.

"Well, Akbar Mohammed Kamal." McKenzie held out his hand. "It's nice to meet you." The boy chuckled and took a hold of McKenzie's hand, shaking it vigorously. "Whoa, steady on half-pint," the Private added with a faux display of pain. "You'll break my hand with that Superman grip!" The boy chuckled harder.

When the hand shaking had ceased, McKenzie held out the harmonica, which Akbar took and studied closely. It was like he had just discovered hidden treasure, running his finger across the embossed chrome casing with extreme care and wonderment.

"Give it a blast half-pint," McKenzie said, making the boy look up with a puzzled expression. McKenzie pointed to the harmonica. "Try it," he encouraged, putting his hand up to his own mouth and blowing into an invisible instrument.

The boy looked back down at the harmonica, paused for a moment and then wiped his lips with the back of his free hand. He held it up to his mouth, pursed his lips and blew, softly.

"Ha-ha, there you go," McKenzie chuckled. "A perfect *G*."

The boy smiled at his achievement and went again, blowing and sucking his way up and down the note holes, getting a little faster and a little louder as his confidence grew.

"You've got some competition there Mickey," Teflon laughed.

"Don't I know it." McKenzie laughed back and began to clap and tap his foot in time to the boy's unlikely rhythm.

The boy continued for a few minutes longer, until the sound of a distance boom put paid to his performance.

"We gotta go boys!" Sergeant Berry called out. "Some shit going on in the Western Quarter apparently."

The boy held out the harmonica towards McKenzie. "Thank you sir," he said. "I enjoy very good."

McKenzie saw the doleful look in the boy's eyes and felt his own wave of sadness. The boy

173

standing before him clearly had nothing in his life other than being involuntarily embroiled in a senseless war that could end his short life.

"Today Mickey!" Teflon shouted impatiently.

"Yeah, yeah, I'm coming!" McKenzie replied taking a step backwards. He pointed at the harmonica in the boy's hand and then at the boy himself. "You keep it half-pint," he said with a smile. "You've earned it." The boy's eyes lit up with delight as McKenzie ruffled his hair, turned around and went to join the others in the MPV.

"You big softy," Aaron teased as McKenzie boarded the vehicle.

Mickey smiled and looked out of the window, just as Akbar Mohammed Kamal began saluting their departure.

*

"Move out of the way Danny." Kyle ordered.

"Yeah?" Danny shot back. "Or what bro'? You gonna smack me like you did your old man?" He squared up to Kyle, his face contorted with rage. "I've known you all my life and you wanna fuck that up just to stop some Paki getting what he deserves?"

"And what does he deserve exactly Danny?" Kyle snapped. "What has he ever done to you, or anybody else for that matter?"

"Have you forgotten what his lot did man? They murdered your fuckin' mum and crippled your sister. You gonna let that slide?"

"He had nothing to do with it you fuckin' retard!" Kyle shouted. "Apart from the fact that he is Turkish, he's not a fuckin' terrorist. What the fuck is wrong with you bro? Where's your head at?"

Danny smiled, shook his head. "It's about fighting back mate," he replied. "Showing them fuckers that we ain't all nicey-nicey and forgivin'. That this is our country and they should follow our rules or fuck off. But, from what I'm seeing, it looks like you've turned into a bit of a pussy bro." He looked to the group standing behind Kyle. "In fact," he went on. "It looks like you've *all* turned into a bunch of pussies!" After a moment's pause, Danny shook his head again, sighed and then took a step backwards, holding up his hands as if conceding to their wishes. "Fine," he shrugged. "If you really wanna leave, go ahead. I ain't gonna stop you." He dropped his hands and then pointed directly at Mehmet. "But the Muslim stays!"

"What?" OD snorted. "How you gonna stop us leaving *with* Mehmet? There are more of us than you dickhead!"

Danny quickly reached into his back pocket, pulled out a black object and held it up for the entire group to see. Nobody was in any doubt what the black object was.

With the push of a small button, a six-inch, steel blade swung out, pointing menacingly towards the group. "Dickhead?" Danny snarled, his face reddening with rage. He suddenly lunged forward, the blade of the flick-knife narrowly missing Kyle's stomach as he and the others moved backwards.

"Danny! What the fuck man?" Kyle shouted.

"Whoa! Put the knife away bro, yeah?" OD called out.

Danny didn't respond; he merely stared at the group, grinned and quickly advanced again, slashing through the air in a frenzied attack.

175

Most of the group managed to retreat quickly down the hallway and back into the relative safety of the living room.

Kyle - on the other hand - didn't.

***

Thirty

Fifty-nine minutes and thirty seconds after exiting the grounds of Angel Court, Firearm Officers arrived at the scene: much to the relief - and surprise - of DI Williams. A heated discussion had already started between him and Mr Yilmaz as the latter's patience had run out and he had insisted on going back into the building.

"Look. Stay here whilst I speak to the Firearms Inspector, yes?" Williams requested. "I will be back to update you in a few minutes."

"As you wish Inspector," Kasim replied with a faint smile.

Williams flicked a suspicious look between Kasim and the silent giant stood by his side. "I'm serious," he added. "Let's not compromise anyone's safety here by trying to play the hero."

"I understand." Kasim replied. "But please," he gestured towards the armed response vehicles. "Can we hurry it along? I have a bad feeling that time is not on our side."

DI Williams nodded and turned to face DC Jackson. "Watch them Jacko," he whispered to his colleague before heading off towards the ARVs.

"Like a hawk." Jackson assured him.

As Williams was returning from his liaison with the armed-unit Inspector, he saw DC Jackson talking on his mobile phone and then noticed something else that made him curse under his breath.

"DC Jackson!" He called out, sharply.

"Yes boss?" Jackson turned quickly towards the advancing inspector.

"Where the fuck has Yilmaz and his cousin gone, *Hawk Eye*?"

*

Youssef put a hand on Kasim's shoulder and stepped forward, indicating that he would enter the building first. Kasim wondered - as he had on so many previous occasions - when Youssef had decided he needed to be a bodyguard. As cousins, they had always looked out for each other but Youssef had clearly proclaimed himself protector. Given his size, it wasn't such a bad thing though.

A few minutes earlier, they had been standing with Detective Jackson who had been instructed - by a not-so-subtle comment from his superior - to keep an eye on them. Much to the irritation of Kasim, the officer was doing his job well: starting an irrelevant conversation and pretending to listen. It appeared that they were stuck with him. But then, Jackson's phone rang. When he withdrew it from his pocket, Kasim noticed the title *Laura XXX* displayed on the bright screen. His girlfriend perhaps, Kasim thought, or sister. Either way, it could turn out to be the opportunity he needed. He just needed to hear the officer's opening words to Laura XXX.

"Excuse me a minute," Jackson said as he turned around to answer the call. "Hi Babe," he said, which was enough to convince Kasim that the call would be sufficiently long.

As Jackson took a few steps away from his wards, Kasim looked at Youssef and nodded. When DI Williams returned, Jackson was still talking on his phone whilst Kasim and Youssef were already at the entrance to Angel Court, on the far side of the building.

"My son is here Youssef," Kasim remarked, "I can sense it." Youssef nodded. "We will head for the second-floor first and hopefully…" He paused and let out a long sigh. "Hopefully, Allah will show us his favour."

*

2nd April 2005. Afghanistan.

The day - as much as any other day in the Helmand Province - had been fraught with skirmishes and pockets of insurgent activity but non more serious than the storming of a government building by Taliban militants in the Deshu district. Three Afghan soldiers had been killed in a two-hour gun battle before the militants finally fled, leaving the security services to mop up the aftermath of destruction.

Sergeant Aaron Berry and his team had been officially tasked with the duty of high-visibility patrol; a detail that consisted of combing the area around the breached government building to deter any immediate threat of further attacks. Unofficially, however, they were ordered to seek out and neutralise four members of the militant group responsible for the attack, who had supposedly taken to hiding themselves in an anti-Taliban residential complex, two miles from the scene. A strange place for a segment of the most hated breed of people in Afghanistan to seek refuge, but maybe that was the point; the security services wouldn't suspect it and the residents would be too frightened to report it.

The intelligence regarding the insurgent's presence had come third hand but - by all accounts - originated from the caretaker of the complex who had reportedly phoned a close friend and pleaded:

They have obviously come here with a purpose and not in peace. I fear for the lives and safety of the families. Please get help before something terrible happens.

When Aaron and his convoy finally arrived, it was gravely apparent that the *terrible* had already happened. Women wailing uncontrollably on the steps whilst men - old and young - quickly surrounded the peacekeepers, shouting, pleading, and frantically pointing towards the building. In a fragmented exchange of languages, Aaron established that a family within the building had been targeted and attacked by the four insurgents. He also established that the incident had occurred on the second floor. What he couldn't establish, was if the aggressors were still in the building or not; a key factor that the terrified and distraught residents couldn't seem to grasp in their eagerness to get help for the targeted family.

"What's the plan sarge?" Teflon asked, whilst the rest of the group listened in.

"The main thing is our safety," Aaron replied. "And I don't intend to rush in there when there is a possibility that the rag-heads are still present and waiting. So, Sully, Pete…" He said, turning to his back-up team leaders. "I want you and your teams to use the emergency stairway and go directly to the fourth floor and start sweeping down. My team will

180

follow you in but break away onto the second floor to see what the situation is there."

"Roger that!" Both team leaders acknowledged.

"Del Boy," Aaron continued, turning to the Sergeant from London's East End. "You and your team secure the ground floor first. Nobody in or out."

"Understood." Del Boy nodded.

"But remember, all of you," Aaron went on. "I personally don't give a fuck about what's gone on inside that building but I do give a fuck about the safety of you lot. So, let's get in there and do our job but let's make sure that we all go home in one piece, yeah?"

A resounding: "Yes sarge!"

"Right," Aaron concluded, glancing at his watch. "Buddy-up and do a quick equipment check and then move out. I want this wrapped up before dark."

*

Angel Court.

Aaron withdrew his hand from the handle of the corridor door and studied it closely. His heart was racing from a rush of adrenaline whilst beads of cold sweat were running down his forehead. He glanced over his shoulder - thankful that nobody had actually followed him up the stairwell - and then refocused on his clammy, shaking hand.

Just anxiety ... flashbacks cause that ... it'll pass soon.

But the flashbacks were happening way too often recently; a condition he thought he had overcome, or could at least control.

He closed his eyes and began to breathe the way his counsellor had shown him: steadily, in through the nose and out through the mouth.

Eventually, Aaron's heart rate slowed and his hand stop shaking enough for him to take hold of the door handle once again. A quick glance through the reinforced, oblong glass panel in the door revealed nothing but darkness beyond. Raising the gun parallel to his face, he slowly pulled the door ajar and was met by a rush of cold, stagnant air: a stench that reminded him of another place from another time.

Aaron's body moved cautiously though the doorway and into the dark of a corridor that was located on the twenty-fourth floor of Angel Court. Aaron's mind however, was back in that place from another time.

*

2nd April 2005. Afghanistan.

The windowless corridor on the second floor of the complex was long and narrow, with the entrance doors of five apartments running along each side. Low wattage bulbs hung from the ceiling at intermittent points, which did little to break through the enforced darkness of the structure. Even when the residents had their front doors open - as appeared to be the case for a couple of apartments halfway down the hallway - the light remained a dirty yellowy-grey, despite the brightness of the day outside.

Gathered around the front door of one of those homes, a few women were sitting on the floor, rocking to and fro as they wailed with grief, whilst others were standing upright with their hands on their faces, almost frozen by whatever they had witnessed. From what Aaron could see, about five men were frantically running in and out of the apartment but appeared to be moving without any real purpose.

"Sit reps?" Sergeant Berry said into his radio, keeping an eye on the group in the corridor. Nobody gave him or his team a second look.

"Four and three, all clear."
"Ground level clear and secured."

Satisfied with the replies from the other teams, Sergeant Berry and his team advanced slowly and precisely, combat rifles held high and at the ready. To presume that the situation in front of them wasn't a trap or potentially volatile would be to ignore all elements of surprise and therefore, compromise safety and lives. Slow and steady was the key.

Trust nothing that you see, trust no one that you meet: Strong words of advice that a Commanding Officer had given Aaron and his comrades on their very first tour of this hellhole.

As the team approached the apartment where all the commotion appeared to have originated from, an Afghani male suddenly came out from the doorway, saw the soldiers and started shouting something unintelligible at them. He then began to close in on the team, pointing back towards the apartment.

"STAY THERE, STAY THERE!" Aaron pointed his rifle directly at the male.

The male either didn't understand the command or chose to ignore it.

"STOP! STAY THERE!" Aaron repeated, and then remembered a piece of what little Arabic he knew. "TARAWUH MAKANAHA!" Stand still.

The man immediately came to a halt, threw his arms into the air but continued shouting. In the broken comprehension of his dialect, Aaron heard two words that he was all too familiar with: *Almadhbuha* and *mayit ... slaughtered* and *dead.*

The man began to walk back towards the apartment, ushering the soldiers on with a wave. Keeping his rifle trained on the man, Aaron slowly advanced, followed closely by his unit. Each soldier was ready to engage should they need to, each soldier was ready for a surprise attack. What the soldiers weren't ready for was what they would encounter in that tiny apartment.

*

Aaron felt his stomach trying to expel its contents when he entered the apartment and witnessed the carnage. He would later describe it to his Commanding Officer as a human abattoir.

The heat in the room had evoked a rancid stench - a combination of sweat and rotting meat - making it almost impossible to breathe. On one of the walls, the word *alkhawna (traitors)* had been written in blood whilst four lifeless bodies - a man, a woman and two children - lay below. The grandmother of the family had been purposely left (relatively) unharmed by the insurgents, thus ensuring that their actions and the consequences of betrayal would be broadcast to others. A cruel legacy in itself but this particular execution had gone way beyond the inhumane.

*

184

It transpired that the assailants - four of them - had entered the building approximately two hours prior to the arrival of the British soldiers and made their way directly to apartment 22 on the second floor. The shouting and screaming that followed alerted every other resident on that floor, with each and every one of them knowing exactly what was about to happen. This wasn't the sound of shouting that sometimes occurs during a family argument; this was a declaration of retribution, of suffering … of imminent death.

The parents, it was said, had been forced onto their knees and then *hog-bound*; arms tied behind their backs and then secured by the same rope to their ankles. Grandmother - frail and in her eightieth year - tried to intervene by grabbing onto the jacket tails of one of the intruders: the one who was barking out the orders. A simple and *mild* swat by the man involved would have been more than sufficient to remove the old woman's grasp but angry insurgents have no concept of that particular adjective. The man looked down at the offending hand, raised his AK47 and brought the butt of it down with ridiculously brute force. The hand shattered as easily as an eggshell dropping to the floor, splinters of bone ripping through the thin, aged skin like it was tissue paper. The old woman moaned in agony; her tired and worn vocal chords negating the ability to produce the scream that such an injury deserved.

The man leant down towards the whimpering matriarch so that his face was just inches away from hers. "In time," he snarled. "Your hand will begin to heal." He moved is mouth closer to her ear. "But I guarantee," he continued in almost a whisper, "such

185

spirit will be broken forever. Just like your ancient heart."

He pulled away slightly and looked her in the eye, his mouth twisted into a sadistic grin. The reaction of the woman - under normal circumstances - would have cost her her life, but on this occasion the man merely grunted, stood upright and wiped the offending spittle from his face.

"Your family," he said, still staring at the old woman. "Have shown disrespect and disloyalty to Allah and his Taliban fighters by engaging in treachery with the infidel British soldiers!"

"Sir. Please," the father pleaded from behind him. "You have been greatly and wrongly misinformed. I beg of you to believe me. We are just …"

"What? Traitors?" The man cut in, turning swiftly around.

"No no, please sir," the father went on. "We are just a poor, God fearing family who have done nothing of what you say. May Allah strike me down if I am lying."

The man appeared to ponder on the father's words before looking over to the corner of the room. He smiled at the two terrified children huddled tightly against each other and held out his hand.

"Come," he said softly. "Sit with your mother and father."

They looked directly at their parents as if seeking permission or advice. Their father hesitated for a moment but, with a heavy heart, nodded his approval.

As they rose from the floor, the man directed them to kneel in front of their parents with a voice that was akin to someone organising a family game

186

of pass-the-parcel. The tone was calm, almost jovial. It was also unnerving.

"Please sir," the knowing father wept. "In the name of Allah and all that is good, please don't hurt my children. They have done nothing. They are just children. Let them witness your mercy, I beg of you."

The man - now standing behind the kneeling son - smiled and began to stroke the child's hair. "I can indeed comprehend the magnitude of mercy," he said. "And have, on occasions, been known to show it."

The father's anxious expression appeared to soften a little, hoping to thank Allah for sparing his son's life.

"Alas," the man went on. "Today is not one of those occasions."

In a swift, controlled movement, the man quickly grabbed the boy's hair, pulled his head backwards and ran a large knife across his throat. The parents screamed in horror as their son's throat opened before them, the main artery severed by the fatal cut. Then - even before the boy's lifeless body had slumped to the floor - the man repeated the same, vicious act on his sister.

The distraught parents barely had enough time to register the cold-blooded murder of their second child, before they were both shot through the back of the head. As if killing them wasn't enough, one of the insurgents tried to behead the father. But - for whatever reason - he had stopped midway, leaving the father's head attached to the body by nothing more than a few sinews of muscle. This needless and senseless attack gave new meaning to the word barbaric.

On 2nd April 2005, members of the Taliban executed two generations of an innocent family without trial…

That was the news; that was the reality.

*

Sergeant Berry had his team remove those in the apartment that were alive and instructed them to prevent anyone - by whatever means - from trying to re-enter. The immediate area had now become a crime scene and despite the residents screaming for answers, protocol still needed to be followed.

Once the front door had been closed - leaving Aaron alone inside - he quickly removed his helmet, rushed into the kitchen area and threw up into the sink, for only the second time in his career. As the nausea subsided, he turned on the cold-water tap and splashed water onto his face. Composure regained, he went back into the main room, took a deep breath and carried on with his job.

The first step was to examine the immediate area around the victims. It wasn't unheard of for insurgents to place an IED beneath a corpse, knowing that the security services would eventually move it and be killed by the ensuing explosion. Aaron wasn't taking any chances on that score.

Slowly and methodically, he searched the bodies of the father, the mother and the girl. All clear. When it came to searching the boy however, Aaron hesitated, noticing the glint of something metallic in the boy's hand. Some form of detonator perhaps?

188

When he had finally and carefully removed the item from the boy's small hand, he studied it for what seemed like an age. And then, Aaron did something that he had never before done in the line of duty: he started to cry.

He eventually turned his attention back to the item he had just recovered and wiped the dried blood from its casing. When he placed it gently back into the boy's hand, the harmonica was almost spotless.

On 2nd April 2005, that was Aaron's news, his reality. It would also become his nightmare.

***

Thirty-One

Angel Court.

When Danny moved forward, Kyle had taken another step back and tried to turn on his heels, but the awkward position of his feet - coupled with the momentum of his body - put him off balance and sent him crashing to the floor. Danny quickly advanced and stood over the fallen youth, pointing the knife towards his torso.

"Not so fuckin' clever now, are you bro?" he snarled, sweeping the blade to and fro.

"Danny, wait!" Kyle shouted. "Think about it, yeah?"

"Oh, I've done nothing but think about this moment," Danny replied. "Because I knew it was coming"

"What does that mean?" Kyle asked, not taking his eyes off the swaying knife.

"You," he answered. He then gestured to the living room with the knife and raised his voice. "And those shithouses in there!"

"Put the knife down Steele!" One of the retreated youths called out. "And we'll see who the shithouse is!"

Danny cackled. "You've all lost your fucking bottle," he spat. "And all because you've suddenly grown a conscience over some worthless Paki!" He looked down and glared at Kyle. "I don't see your little Muslim mate rushing out to help you now bro, do you? Seems to me like he's sacrificing you to save his own arse. But what did you expect, hanging around with his type? They're just a bunch of Allah's bitches, waiting to blow shit up. And that's the problem with this weak, do-good country. No fucker wants to fight back!"

"And you know what your problem is Danny?" Kyle replied, glaring up at him

Danny frowned. "What, genius?"

"You talk way too fucking much!"

Before Danny could react, Kyle seized the opportunity he had seen manifest itself as Danny preached his anger. Unfortunately for Danny, his legs had straddled Kyle's, leaving the latter with room enough to manoeuvre with ease. In one swift movement, Kyle flung his leg upwards, the lower part of his shin making perfect contact with Danny's exposed groin area. Danny groaned with shocked pain and doubled over, affording Kyle more space to retract both his legs and kick out towards Danny's chest. Danny flew backwards, allowing Kyle to rise to his feet and advanced on him with a roar. Danny blindly raised the knife up in front of himself but Kyle was too quick, taking hold of Danny's wrist to prevent the knife being thrust out. Within seconds, the pair was in close combat, each trading one armed blows and knee strikes in a bid to weaken the other and gain the upper hand. Kyle wondered how much longer he could hold on to Danny's wrist: Danny knew that it wouldn't be long but then again, he didn't expect the sudden and painful jar that Kyle inflicted by bending his wrist back on itself. The knife dropped from Danny's grip and fell to the floor, giving Kyle a chance to kick it away with his foot. Danny - both arms now free - gripped onto Kyle's lapels, pulled him sharply inwards and head butted

191

the bridge of his nose; the loud snap was enough confirmation that it was broken. Kyle yelped and staggered backwards, holding his hands up to his face. Had it not been for the hallway wall directly behind him, he would have surely dropped to the ground once again.

Danny quickly turned away from Kyle, reached down and retrieved the knife from the floor. As he turned back around, he had no time compute - or block - the unexpected flying kick that connected squarely with his torso and sent him onto the seat of his pants. Winded, he looked up to see OD - who had raced from the lounge to help Kyle - bearing down on him, already releasing another kick. Danny somehow managed to tilt his head sideways and avoid the impact of OD's foot by millimetres but OD was quick to follow up with a punch to his temple. Fortunately for Danny, most of the power in the punch had been dampened by the kinetics of the missed kick and the resulting effect was minimal. Unfortunately for OD, his body was now inches away from Danny, who still had the knife in his grip. Danny swung his arm and plunged the knife into OD's arm: not enough to be fatal but certainly enough to cause extreme pain. OD howled and staggered back, holding his pierced, bloody arm. Danny jumped to his feet and snarled. "Come on then, you fucking Muppets. Who's hard enough now?"

OD went to move forward but Kyle stepped in front of him and faced Danny. "This has gone far enough man," he said. "It needs to stop, now."

Danny grinned. "It stops when I fuckin' say so Roberts," he replied. "I ain't your bitch, like the rest of them pussies!"

"No." OD spat. "You're a fuckin' psycho with a knife!"

Danny shrugged. "I just hope you boys are halal flavoured?" He cackled, whilst OD and Kyle frowned.

"What the fuck are you on about, you dick?" Kyle demanded.

Danny's features instantly changed to a twisted expression of rage. "You two nob 'eds," he hissed, pointing the blade towards Kyle and OD. "Are gonna get cut up into little pieces and fed to your pet Muslim." He raised the knife, ready to attack. "COME ON!" he shouted, like a battle cry.

As he stepped forward, only Kyle and OD saw the giant Asian man enter the front door behind Danny, both in silent awe of the stealth and speed of such a huge bloke.

The first that Danny knew about Youssef's presence was when a thick arm suddenly wrapped itself around his neck and deftly placed him into a chokehold.

And the second? Well, from Danny's perspective nobody knew, because he was now being lowered to the ground having been rendered unconscious.

Youssef took the knife from Danny's limp hand, stood up and stepped to one side, allowing Kasim to make an appearance.

"Where is my son?" Was all he asked.

*

In the dark of a corridor two floors up, Aaron listened intently to the sound of raised voices, trying to pinpoint the direction of the source. In an old abandoned building - with broken windows and missing doors - the ears can easily be deceived. Sounds can carry on the wind and resound off bare walls, changing direction and tone in an instant. But it wasn't just Aaron's ears that were being deceived; it was his mind too, consumed by the replay of dark memories. So, when the injured screech of OD bounced and echoed its way from the melee inside flat 220, up two floors and into Aaron's ears, his mind deciphered it as the sound of a fellow soldier calling out for help. Somewhere within that building of slaughter, a brother needed help and he needed it now.

Aaron couldn't comprehend why the soldiers just beyond him weren't responding nor why their statures appeared to be a little blurred. He frowned with confusion but decided to address the inexplicable disappointment later. Now though, he needed to go.

"I'll check it out," he said into the empty darkness. "You lot stand fast here!"

Aaron checked his weapon, turned quickly on his heels and headed back towards the stairwell.

***

Thirty-Two

"Dad?"

The voice was undeniable. Kasim immediately marched along the hallway whilst Kyle and OD quickly stepped aside to allow his passage.

"Mehmet," he cried out with noticeable relief once he'd entered the living room and seen his son.

"DAD!" Mehmet gasped and almost ran into his father's arms. Kasim embraced him in a way that Mehmet had never before experienced from his father and it felt good. "I'm so sorry Dad," he whispered, tearfully. "Please, forgive me?"

"No, no, no," Kasim replied softly. "It is I who should be sorry. I have failed you as a father and protector and I only hope that *you* can forgive *me*?"

When they eventually broke their hug, Mehmet stepped back and for the first time, saw that his dad was crying. "You have done nothing to be sorry for papa," he consoled.

Kasim's expression suddenly changed from one of relief to one of concern. "Oh my god," he gasped, studying his son's face. "What have they done to you?" He took a gentle hold of Mehmet's chin and turned his head one way and then the other, noting the cuts and bruises on his son's face. He looked around at the others in the room. "Who did this?" He growled. "And what is the meaning of that?" He pointed towards the video camera still set up and facing towards an empty chair.

Nobody in that room dared speak. Not for the first time during this whole debacle, the group knew

195

what Aaron had planned for Mehmet was wrong: but now? The realisation - and the guilt - seemed to be compounded. It was as if their eyes had only just become fully open to how bad this situation actually was and no words could possibly make it any better … or justify it.

Kasim studied the *stage* with angry contempt and an overwhelming urge to lash out. Turning to a small table, he noticed a piece of paper lying on it and cast his eyes over the text. When he had finished reading, he glared at the youths standing awkwardly in the room and asked: "Which one of you is Aaron?"

The group couldn't answer fast enough. After all, they had just been given an opportunity to lay blame elsewhere and perhaps save their own skins.

When Kasim was eventually told who and where Aaron was - and why - the only action he needed to concentrate on now was getting his son out of that building and fast.

*

Out in the stairwell of Angel Court - now just one floor up - *Sergeant* Aaron Berry was cautiously making his way down to the twenty-second floor, ready to engage with any insurgent that dared show their face.

*

Outside of the building, DI Williams had been using all his powers of persuasion and reasoning to convince the Firearms Inspector to send his team of armed Police Officers into Angel Court after Kasim and his cousin.

"I'm not altogether happy with this shit Andy." The Firearm Inspector said. "If it goes tits-up, we're *all* in the sticky brown stuff, right up to our necks!"

"Then let's make sure it doesn't," Andy replied. "Because if it does Jeff, it won't just be the curly-finger into some Super's office we'll have to face, it'll be a grilling in coroner's court and a witch-hunt by the Internal Affair wanks!"

"Fuck me Andy," Jeff said with a wry smile. "You got anymore motivational speeches to share?"

Williams laughed. "Yeah, I'm glad it's you lot going in there and not me."

That particular conversation had taken place approximately five minutes before the sound of a gunshot rang out for the second time that evening. And then, moments later, a third report was added.

It appeared that the situation inside Angel Court might have already gone *tits-up*.

***

Thirty-Three

Danny slowly opened his eyes and allowed them to focus before eventually sitting up. His head throbbed whilst his throat felt as though somebody had attached a fucking vice to it. He touched it and grimaced at the tenderness. Not good.

In his disorientation, the sound of unfamiliar voices coming from another room temporarily confused him, but then - faster than the dissipation of breath on a cold pane of glass - the mist cleared and his senses returned … as did his anger.

Taking stock of the situation, he saw that he had been put into what appeared to be a bedroom but right now, that wasn't a concern. What was a concern, was finding out what shithouse had sneaked up on him from behind and laid him out. Once he knew that, he could address the problem head on and kick the fuck out of them. Clearly he had no idea that Youssef was the alleged *shithouse*.

He stood up way too fast, became lightheaded and almost dropped back down again, but managed to steady himself against the wall and eventually find his balance. Taking a breath, he headed towards the door, determined to find out what exactly was going on. Time was being wasted with all this fucking chatter and things needed to move along.

Although he didn't know why, Danny cautiously opened the bedroom door, just enough to be able to peer through the gap and see what was happening beyond the room he was in. Just then, some stocky Asian bloke - who Danny didn't

198

recognise - marched past the room, followed by another, much smaller Asian man.

"What the fuck?" He muttered to himself. "I've woken up in a fuckin' mosque!"

The initial bewilderment quickly turned itself back into anger when - seconds later - he watched Mehmet also passing by.

Danny suddenly yanked open the door and stepped into the hallway, almost getting himself mown down by the rest of the group following Mehmet.

"Move Steele!" Kyle spat, pushing Danny to one side.

"What the fuck's going on?" Danny barked. "You're letting the Paki escape!"

"Get back in your fuckin' hole, dick head!" OD shouted and pushed Danny back into the room he had just egressed from. Still feeling weak from his earlier induced sleep, Danny slumped to the floor and watched on helplessly as the other members of the group - Mally and Wing Nut - headed for the front door too.

The adrenaline from the rage that was now spilling over from inside Danny's mind caused him to jump back onto his feet as though he had been hit with a high-voltage charge from a defibrillator.

"Not a fucking chance he's leaving!" Danny hissed. "No way!"

As he quickly stomped after the group, he couldn't help but wonder - with all this rebellion shit going down - where the fuck Aaron was.

*

Outside, the rainclouds in the night sky had finally drifted apart, allowing the moon to show her face in all its glory. Like the beam of a spotlight from a hovering search helicopter, the side of Angel Court was suddenly lit up by the moon's brilliance. Shafts of white seeped in through broken windows and sprayed an eerie glow across the inner walls.

In the stairwell - just between the twenty-third and twenty-second floor - Aaron quickly stepped back from out of the unexpected radiance and disappeared into the dark shadows of a corner. It was what he had been trained to do.

He waited patiently in position knowing from the sound of the footsteps that the enemy was heading his way and would come out through the only door available to them. He had them cornered and it was just a matter of time until the target emerged. His breathing was slow and controlled, his mind focused, his hand steady. He was ready to do his job.

Seconds later, the stairwell door opened and a well-built Asian held it back whilst a much smaller Asian man came through followed by an Asian youth.

Insurgents?

Aaron wasted no time.

"STOP!" he shouted and fired a warning shot into the wall above their heads.

The scene was freeze framed as Aaron stepped forward from the cover of the shadow and held his gun in a firing position. Whilst three Turkish Muslims stood rigid, four British youths - still in the neighbouring hallway - retreated back from the doorway to seek cover. None of them paid any attention to Danny, who had now caught up and was passing them, but then again, Danny didn't pay any attention to them either. All he was interested in was grabbing hold of Mehmet, who he could see in the doorway with his back turned. "Gotcha, you little fucker!" He muttered to himself, with a vague sense a victory.

Out in the stairwell, Youssef grunted and took half a step towards Aaron but Kasim put a hand on his arm and shook his head.

"Wanna try your luck raghead?" Aaron invited with a glare, whilst applying a little more pressure to the trigger.

Suddenly, there was an unexpected yell from the corridor just beyond the open door. Aaron quickly shifted his eyes and trained his weapon directly onto Mehmet, just as Mehmet turned his head sideways and made as though he was about to make a run for it. Sergeant Berry fired his gun in rapid response. Shoot to kill. No hesitation, no second warning. It was what he had been trained to do.

Without doubt, the Grim Reaper had already inscribed the recipient's name on the bullet that left Aaron's firearm and it probably read: *RIP Mehmet Kasim*.

***

Thirty-Four

"Go, go, go!"

The Firearms Sergeant waved some of his men forward whilst another section remained in position, covering the entrance and windows of Angel Court. When the first group of armed officers arrived at the entrance door, the second section quickly followed, their weapons trained on the empty flats above just in case any threat suddenly presented itself from there.

Under the relative safety of the entrance door overhang, Sergeant Blake addressed the team.

"Right. You know the script lads, we've ran this scenario a million times in training, yes?"

"Sarge." Came the unified agreement.

"When we go in there, let's find our target as quickly as possible and, if necessary, take him down. Most importantly, watch your backs and cover the backs of those in front of you. Let's be sure that we are all going home safe gents." The group nodded their acknowledgement. "Now," Blake continued. "As soon as we open this door, it's hand signals only. The less noise we make the more we will hear and the less likely it is that the target will catch on to our approach." Satisfied that his team fully understood the order of play, he gave a nod to the officer who had his hand poised on the door handle: the signal to enter the building and face the unexpected.

When they reached the seventh floor, the unexpected happened.

*

For what seemed like an eternity, nobody moved; too shocked to react in any way, shape or form, as they stared in horror at the lifeless body slumped on the crumbling concrete floor.

A small ocean of deep crimson had immediately flowed from the youth's head and was now connecting with the shoes of some of the onlookers, but they were too stunned to even notice.

The bullet from Aaron's gun had entered the base of the skull, shattering bone like it was a delicate meringue. It had then ripped through the soft brain tissue but had come to an abrupt stop as it lodged itself in the right cheekbone of the victim. The tip of the bullet could actually be seen, pushing against the skin from inside out like some miniature alien embryo trying to break out from its cocoon. Death was instantaneous, which was probably a good thing for the deceased, although death wasn't something that the rest of the group would have wished on anybody … including Danny.

*

Whether it had been an intervention by some heavenly body, pure bad luck - or good luck, depending on who you were - or just a cruel hand of fate, nobody could deny that Danny's demise was wholly ironic.

He had gone after Mehmet with a head full of rage and eyes full of hate, his mind so clouded by red mist that he probably didn't even hear the first gunshot ring out. So, when he saw Mehmet standing in the doorway like a statue, he saw it as his opportunity to pounce on the fucker, hold him down and stop his pending escape. Aaron would be well made up. He might even let him be the cameraman, once he had told him about the others shitting out. Danny felt good about himself.

He sprinted up the corridor and literally dived towards Mehmet; a millisecond before Aaron discharged his gun once again. The momentum of Danny's body knocked Mehmet to one side, but subsequently put his own head in the direct path of the airborne bullet's trajectory. In short, Mehmet was actually saved from death whilst Danny took the bullet.

*

The first person to say something was Mally, but there were only two words he could actually manage before throwing up: *Oh* and *Shit.*

Kyle drew in a large breath and glared at Aaron. "What the fuck have you done?" He screamed. Aaron stared back at him blankly. "You fuckin' shot him you retard!" Kyle added. "He's fuckin' dead man, DEAD!"

Aaron frowned, looked down at the gun in his hand and then slowly back to Danny's corpse. Suddenly, he let out an exasperated gasp of honest surprise tainted with pure horror. It was as though he had just been dragged back from past times and into the here and now; a journey that had resulted in confusion and despair and it wasn't good. In fact, the whole situation - and him - was truly fucked up. He sat down on the step, held his head in his hands and began to hit the hilt of the gun hard against his forehead.

"Aaron? AARON?" Kyle shouted but there was clearly nothing registering.

204

"We need to go, now!" Kasim urged. "Come Mehmet, quickly."

Mehmet remained transfixed on the body of Danny, his own body trembling whilst silent tears ran down his face.

"Mehmet!" Kasim called with a more forceful tone.

Slowly - yet painfully - Mehmet turned to his father, opened his mouth as though he was about to speak but said nothing. Kasim's face softened into an expression of understanding and love: as a parent's does when their children are hurting.

"It's okay son," he offered, with a soft tone. "Come," he added, gesturing with his hand. "It's time to leave."

Mehmet began to move towards his father just as Aaron shot up off the step and pointed his gun at the group once more.

At that moment, every person in that group wondered which one of them would be assassinated next but none of them expected Aaron's next move.

"The man's right," he said, matter-of-factly. "You all need to leave." Nobody moved a muscle. "NOW!" Aaron shouted, waving the gun "Go on. Fuck off, all of you!"

This time, nobody needed to be told again. The group started down the stairs with great urgency, just in case the high probability of Aaron changing his mind again came into play. Nobody wanted to be around for that.

When they had all disappeared from view, Aaron let his arm holding the gun drop to one side, sat back down on the step and held his head in his hands. A few minutes of silent reflection later, he looked up and sighed.

"Why are you still here Kyle?"

***

Thirty-Five

At first, it sounded like the rumble of distant thunder but the sound remained constant and was gradually getting louder, closer.

The lead officer held up his hand and the group following in his wake halted immediately, weapons trained on both the space above them and the space below. Sergeant Blake made his way up to the lead officer who signalled for him to listen and pointed upwards.

At first - with the steady breeze outside humming its way in through the broken windowpanes - the sound was difficult to decipher. It appeared to be coming from way above their third-floor position but then again - in a building where sounds are twisted and manipulated by emptiness - it could have been coming from anywhere.

And then, the sound stopped.

Sergeant Blake frowned and listened some more but the sound had definitely ceased.

Eventually, he nodded to the lead officer, signalled to the team behind him and they all continued to advance, quickly engulfed by the darkness beyond.

*

When Kyle was a boy, he would live for the days when Aaron came to visit. Aside from his mum, Aaron was the best adult that Kyle had ever known *and* he was a soldier.

Regardless of whatever was going on in Aaron's life, he would always spend quality time with Kyle; whether that was kicking a ball about, sitting through Kyle's many *magic* shows or just chatting about things that were important to a four-year-old boy. He was the ideal role model: unlike his brother-in-law who was a total waster and way out of his sister's league.

Whenever Angela informed her son that uncle Aaron was on leave and due to visit, Kyle would make sure that his Action Man, Lego set or magic kit was accessible way before Aaron's arrival and then sit on the couch, staring out of the window and down the garden path. In Kyle's eyes, Aaron was king.

However. In 2005 Aaron's visits became less and less frequent and when he did visit, Kyle noticed a change in the man he had once seen as his second dad. The change was subtle at first but, as all children do, Kyle sensed that all was not well. Whenever he'd asked his mum what was wrong with uncle Aaron, she would always reply with the same stock answer that parents give to their inquisitive and sensitive offspring in such situations.

"Oh, nothing darling. He's just a bit tired, that's all."

Trouble was, the older Kyle got the more he saw just how *tired* Aaron was becoming and so - whenever Aaron made one of his rare visits - Kyle would stay in his room or go out with friends.

The situation not only worried Kyle, it hurt like hell, as for the first time in his relatively short life, he began to feel fatherless.

*

208

"What the fuck happened to you Aaron?" Kyle asked, trying hard not to break.

Aaron stared at Kyle through soulless eyes, eyes that were void of emotion; eyes - Kyle thought - that looked dead.

"When your mother was…"

"Don't you fuckin' dare try to blame this shit on my mum's death!" Kyle snapped, surprised by his own anger yet compelled to continue. It was *his* time to vent. "My mum had no chance at that concert and I miss her every single minute of the day but that doesn't give me or anybody else the right to start killing people. Yeah, I'm as angry as fuck that some fuckin' psycho took her life and almost ended my sister's, but going round kidnapping people just because they have the same colour skin as that terrorist? Murdering them in the name of vengeance? Nah mate. That makes you just as bad as they are, worse even." He looked down towards the corpse. "Danny was a fuckin' idiot but he didn't deserve to die bro!"

"It was an accident." Aaron replied, defensively. "I didn't mean to shoot…"

"No, you didn't mean to shoot him," Kyle cut in aggressively. "You meant to shoot Mehmet, so don't try and justify what you did by saying it was an accident. That's just fucked up!"

"I *am* fucked up!" Aaron bit back. "But what would you know about it? You're just a kid with no fucking idea about the real world!"

"Well, if this is the real world." Kyle replied. "I don't want anything to do with it!"

"Piss off then." Aaron said. "No fucker is asking you to stay!"

"Believe me I would." Kyle began. "If I didn't think you needed help and you weren't family. But you do and you are, so…"

"So what?" Aaron spat. "What the fuck can you do about anything? You couldn't even wipe your own arse a few years ago so what help are you to me now?" He suddenly stood up from the step he was sitting on and - unnervingly - began to wave his gun back and forth. "It's people like me that help you and all the other spineless fuckers in this country, not the other way round. I sit on that fucking wall day and night, protecting your freedom, your right to live and how do we get repaid? With a pat on the back and some worthless fuckin' medal!" He stepped towards Kyle and Kyle immediately saw that same lost expression returning to Aaron's face.

"Put the gun down man, yeah?" Kyle tried.

Aaron didn't seem to register the sentence but worse still, he didn't seem to register that it was his own nephew in front of him.

"We are in a fucking war here my friend," he continued. "And people like him?" He looked down at Danny and gave a small shrug. "Collateral damage." He added, matter-of-factly. "A victim of the battle we are fighting against terrorism, both domestic and international. Unavoidable? Maybe. But that isn't the real question here, is it?" He turned back to Kyle and scowled. "The *real* question is…" He leaned in towards Kyle and lowered his voice to a dark hiss. "Are you with me or against me?"

He studied Kyle's expression for what seemed like an eternity and though Kyle never spoke a word, Aaron nodded and blew out a dismissive breath. "Thought so," he said.

In a quick and wholly unexpected move, Aaron suddenly grabbed Kyle by the throat, forced him back against the wall and pressed the barrel of the gun against the centre of his forehead.

Kyle wanted to scream - protest, fight back - but fear had seemingly severed his vocal chords and erased his motor skills. At that moment in time, Kyle could do nothing but wait for what he assumed was the inevitable.

*

The group had literally sprinted down seven flights of stairs, jogged down a further four flights and had now adopted a walking pace for the remainder but only because the amount of unseen hazards hiding in the dark of the stairwell dictated it so.

As they approached level seven, Mehmet glanced backwards and then frowned. "Wait," he called out, bringing everyone to a halt. "Where's Kyle?" Everyone gave a cursory glance back up the stairwell followed by a few uneasy shrugs.

"I thought he was behind you," Mally said to his brother.

"I thought he was too," OD replied, feeling both mystified and guilty that he hadn't even noticed Kyle's absence. "I'll go back and look for him."

"No," Kasim said directly. "We need to get out of here now. There is no telling what that crazy man will do and whatever has happened to Kyle, has happened."

"And there's nothing we can do about it?" OD asked, with a bitter tone. "Is that what you're sayin'?"

"I am saying that it is better that we all get outside first and let he Police deal with it."

"What? Like you did for him?" OD challenged, nodding towards Mehmet. "*Let the Police deal with it?*"

"That's different." Kasim replied. "He's my son."

"And Kyle is my mate." OD argued.

Kasim shrugged and let out a sigh. "It's a pity that you didn't think about that before you and your stupid acquaintances here, dragged him into something way above your limited intelligence."

OD quickly stepped forward, clearly intending to square up to Kasim. Youssef quickly sideways, blocking his progress. OD looked Youssef up and down with utter disdain whilst Youssef merely raised his eyebrows: a non-verbal communication that said: *try if you dare.*

OD made the correct decision to step back and raised his hands in submissive understanding. "Fine," he said. "You've got your precious son now so, go on, fuck off. But just remember that it was Kyle who came to help Mehmet!"

"And should I be thankful?" Kasim replied. "Should I perhaps kneel and give praise to Allah that my son was helped by a boy whose own family and friends put him through this ordeal in the first place?" Kasim hissed a sardonic laugh. "No, I think not," he continued. "And if you believe that I should have empathy for Kyle or that I will harbour any guilt by not going back up those stairs to help you find him, then you are more stupid than I'd originally thought, which wasn't flattering to begin with."

OD opened his mouth to reply but then something on Kasim's jacket caught his eye. A small, yet intensely bright red dot had suddenly appeared on his chest, positioned directly where his heart would be.

OD frowned and pointed towards Kasim. "What the fuck is that?" He quizzed, and though Kasim looked down, he had no opportunity to reply.

"ARMED POLICE. GET DOWN. GET DOWN NOW!"

The invisible voice bellowed from within the shroud of darkness on the stairs below them, followed by the illumination of more red dots, dancing in the dark until they eventually found their spots … on the hearts of every other person within the group.

"ON THE FLOOR NOW!" Another command.

"DOWN, DOWN, DOWN!" Came another.

Not until the group's brains had finally registered what was going on and they had begun to comply, did the owners of the assertive voices ascend from the cover of blackness. Speedily and precisely, the armed officers advanced, grabbing hold of those that hadn't fully grasped the concept of getting down onto the floor and forcing them into a prone position.

For a reason that even Wing Nut couldn't explain, he suddenly found the audacity to voice his protest and subsequently received a painful reminder of who was in charge.

"Say one more fucking word," the cop growled. "I dare you!"

Wing Nut declined the dare for two reasons. The first was that he had had the wind knocked out of him and the second - and more important reason - is that he had the barrel of a sub-machine gun pointing at his forehead. So, no thanks PC Angry, I'll pass on that dare.

Within a matter of minutes, Kasim, Youssef, Mehmet, OD, Mally and Wing Nut were all on their knees, hands tied behind their backs with strong plastic pull-ties.

Sergeant Blake shone his flashlight onto the face of Youssef and then onto Kasim. "Mister Yilmaz I presume?" Kasim nodded. Blake sighed and shook his head. "There's a reason you were told to stay outside," he went on. "You're lucky that we don't have any over-enthusiastic or twitchy-fingered officers in our team. Things could have turned out pretty badly for you lot."

"I just needed to get to my son," Kasim whispered. "If you're a father, you should understand that?"

Blake remained silent for a while. He was a father - to three beautiful children - but he wasn't going to share that information. He focused his torch on Mehmet and felt an unusual pang of sympathy wash over him. It looked like the boy had been through some tough shit already. He hadn't deserved it but Manchester was living in anxious times, times when the dregs of society feel they have a justifiable right to commit violent acts against those that they deem to be different. It's been the same throughout the city's history. HIV? Victimise the gay community. Ebola? Victimise the African community. An attack on the Arena? Victimise the Muslims community. In the minds of fools everybody else is to blame for the crap that happens in the world and their only answer? Intimidation, harassment and persecution of minorities: an evil formula that millions of second-world wartime Jews recall with dread.

Blake nodded to one of his colleagues. "Take these three out," he instructed, pointing to Mehmet, Kasim and Youssef.

"Hey?" OD piped up. "What about us?"

"Shut up dick!" Blake spat. "You go if and when we say you can go. In the meantime, we've a lot to talk about, starting with who's still up there and why? Got it?" OD stared at him blankly. "I'll take that as a yes." Blake continued. "Right then. Somebody tell me what the fuck is going on?"

***

Thirty-Six

"Is this what you want? You want me to shoot you because you'd rather side with *them*?"

It was Aaron that held Kyle against the wall yet Kyle didn't recognise him. When would Aaron ever have considered playing out this shit? Never in a million years Kyle had thought, yet here he was, pressing a loaded gun into his nephew's forehead with more than a mild inclination to pull the trigger.

"Is that what *you* want?" Kyle responded. "You want to murder your own flesh and blood?"

"Don't fuckin' twist this round bro. You're the one betraying your own family."

"How the fuck am I doing that Aaron?" Kyle's initial fear turned into anger. "I've lost my mum because some fuck-wit decided he was gonna play executioner in the name of his belief and here you are, about to do the same."

"The same? How is this the same? I'm not killing innocent people!"

"Really!" Kyle snapped. "Tell that to fuckin' Danny!"

Aaron looked towards Danny's body and frowned as though it was the first time he'd seen it. Without speaking, without taking his eyes off the shattered, bloody skull of the corpse, Aaron released his grip of Kyle and lowered the gun.

Kyle frowned. "Aaron?" He said, but there was nothing. "Aaron?" he repeated, a little louder.

Aaron finally turned back to Kyle; the previous look of anger and hate on his face replaced by a genuine expression of anguish.

"What the fuck have I done bro?" He whispered.

Kyle studied his uncle with a little uncertainty, wondering if this change of emotion was genuine or just another play. When Aaron's eyes glazed and then expelled tears, Kyle was still not wholly convinced. "Aaron?" he tried. "Give me the gun man."

Aaron frowned, looked uneasily at the gun in his hand and then over towards Danny "Oh shit, what have I done?" he repeated softly, almost to himself.

Without really thinking about it, Kyle placed his hand gently onto Aaron's and manoeuvred it so that the barrel of the gun was pointing down. "It's okay mate," he said. "Just give me the gun, yeah?"

Aaron turned and studied the hand on top of his.

Never give up your weapon private! ... The advice was distant but very clear: as clear as the first day of basic training.

"Aaron, give me the gun?"

Unless you fancy being shot by your own gun.

"Aaron?"

Aaron shook his head slightly - 'Just memories fucking with my head,' he thought.

Not just memories son, a code.

Aaron clenched his jaw tightly and slowly began to loosen his grip on the gun.

Don't you fucking do it soldier!

"That's it mate." Kyle encouraged. "No drama."

Never - NEVER - give up your weapon!

"Aargh!" Aaron hissed and began slapping the side of his own head with his free hand. "Fuck off!"

"What?" Kyle asked, confused and concerned by the sudden display.

You gonna give him your weapon, after all you've been taught?

"Yes … No … I just …"

"Aaron. What is it man?"

He will shoot you!

Aaron shut his eyes tightly, hoping - praying - that he could get a grip on reality. But what was real anyway? Where was the line between then and now?

When he eventually opened his eyes, he gasped at the sight of a young boy standing in the doorway of the stairwell. Although the boy was smiling, teardrops hung onto his dirty cheeks, as if frozen in time. In his hand he appeared to be holding on to something tightly - like it was new found treasure he didn't want to lose - and though Aaron couldn't actually see what it was, he was inexplicably drawn to it. Without words, the boy slowly extended his arm and opened his hand to reveal what had gotten the better of Aaron's curiosity. And there - resting on the boy's small palm with accentuated clarity - was a battered and blood stained harmonica.

*

"Jesus. What was that?"

Sergeant Blake looked up into the stairwell and shone his torch into the wall of black.

The sound that had bounced its way down from the floors above was like the cry of a banshee. It was piercing, it was loud and it was very unsettling.

218

Then, there was an echo of what sounded like a door being slammed hard, followed by the sound of footsteps running down the concrete stairs towards them.

Blake looked back towards his team. "Right, he began. "You two take this lot out. The rest of you, with me."

*

The scream was unlike any other that Kyle had ever heard, as terrifying as the sound effects of a horror movie.

Aaron yanked his hand away from Kyle's, stepped back and pointed the gun back at his nephew.

"No Aaron, please." Kyle begged, trembling with fear. "Don't shoot me!"

Aaron's face was ashen; a mixture of horror, confusion and sadness embedded in an expression that - like the scream - Kyle had never witnessed before. If there was an image that conveyed the complete and utter breakdown of the mind and soul, then Aaron's face had to be it.

Kyle knew that there was no reasoning or bargaining with his uncle anymore and he doubted that Aaron even recognised him right now. This was it, he thought. This was the way that his life was going to end. Shot with a gun held by his kin, in some decrepit, condemned shit hole.

Kyle closed his eyes and tried to convince himself that his slayer-to-be wasn't his uncle - the man who he had admired and adored for most of his life - but some random psychotic stranger whom Kyle had unfortunately stumbled upon. Sadly, the majority of that thought was now closer to the truth than Kyle had imagined.

Kyle was expecting the shot. What he wasn't expecting was the sudden and forceful shove to his arm that sent him stumbling sideways. He immediately opened his eyes and found his balance just in time to see Aaron heading back towards the direction of his flat.

"Aaron, wait!" he called out.

"You need to fuck off Kyle," Aaron shouted back. "Whilst you still can!"

"No, wait, wait!" Kyle tried again, but the only reply he received was the loud thud of a door being slammed shut.

Kyle was temporarily suspended in decision limbo. Should he go after his uncle and try talking to him again or should he just fuck off and not risk getting killed?

And then, in a moment of unforeseen clarity, another thought struck him; a thought that was so plausible - so obvious, so real - that it horrified him to the core.

With an overwhelming sense of urgency, Kyle immediately turned around and headed for the stairwell.

***

Thirty-Seven

Aaron locked and bolted the door behind him. He didn't want his nephew barging in trying to convince him that help was at hand or worse, continue to peck his head about surrendering the gun.

Never give up your weapon!

"I didn't did I?" he snapped. "So fuck off!"

Not content with the deadlocks and bolts on his door, Aaron piled whatever items he could find against it and then did the same with the living room door, once he had closed that too. He had shit to sort and he didn't want anybody interfering with his plans.

He stood behind the video camera, opened out the LCD viewing panel and powered it up, making sure that the chair in front of the camera lens was dead centre of the small screen. Satisfied, he picked up a sheet of paper from a side table, quickly scanned the text and then took up his position; centre stage.

Aaron glanced once more at the paper he was holding, cleared his throat and then looked up into the camera lens.

"People of Great Britain," he began. "We have all witnessed way too many attacks on the innocent citizens of our nation by those who believe that it is God's will."

"Some of you have seen your loved ones injured or murdered by the cowardly actions of those fighting in the name of Islam, twisting the true meaning of their prophets to justify their barbaric carnage."

"On the twenty second of May, twenty-two people, including my own sister, were taken from us; my niece disabled and confined to a wheelchair. And for what? Because they were soldiers? Because they were at war with ISIS? No. It was because they *dared* to be at a pop concert. Not an anti-Taliban rally, not some protest against Allah, but a simple pop concert where they and many others like them were guilty of nothing more than enjoying themselves!"

Aaron paused and looked down at the floor: a moment to compose himself.

He glanced at the sheet of paper still in his hand, shook his head and tossed it to one side.

When he looked back up and into the camera, his expression was clearly remorseful. "I have done something very wrong," he continued quietly. "Something unforgiveable."

"I guess I needed to make somebody accountable for my sister's death. Make an example of them; make them appreciate how much I'm hurting, how much her children are hurting and how much the families of the other victims are hurting. I just needed to try and make some kind of fuckin' sense of it all."

"I only set out to scare someone, shake them up a little, make them feel as shit as I do … I had no intention of..."

"I know that vengeance isn't the answer; it's just an excuse for violence. I know it yet I ignored it and I got lost in this crazy fucking notion that I could restore some sort of balance."

"And now, because of me, some poor lad has lost his fucking life and that …that makes me just as bad as they are!"

222

Aaron looked away from the active video camera to try and hide his emotion. After a few moments, he wiped his eyes, took a deep breath and turned back.

"I can't change what I've done," he went on, eventually. "And I know that nothing I can say will ever make the people that I've hurt, forgive me. But who the fuck would blame them? Not me. I can't even forgive myself!"

"If I could turn back the clock then…"

Then what? You wouldn't have ended Danny's life? Too late for that shit soldier!

"IF I could turn back the clock…"

Forget it. What's done is done. Collateral damage, that's all.

"No, no it isn't. He was just a boy, just a fucking boy!"

Aaron forgot that the video recorder was still capturing every moment, because - without a second thought - he put his head into his hands and sobbed.

When he eventually found control, he wiped his hands across his face and looked directly at the gun he had placed onto the small table.

You know what needs to be done now, don't you?

Aaron hesitated for just a moment and then took in another deep breath.

"Yeah," he whispered. "I know."

***

Thirty-Eight

The last ten hours had dragged: questions followed by more questions followed by even more questions.

Kyle didn't blame the cops for wanting to know what the fuck had gone on over the last twenty-four hours and why - after all, it was their job - but he just wished they'd leave him alone; for a little while at least.

"The sooner we have all the facts, the sooner we can consider our options." DI Williams said. "But until then, I'm gonna ask you over and over again about this because your mates…"

"They're not my mates." Kyle interrupted sharply. "Not anymore."

"Okay then," Williams went on. "Your *former* mates, seem intent on putting all the blame onto someone who isn't here to defend themselves and I for one, think they're full of shit. There was a clear conspiracy to cause harm to Mehmet Yilmaz that's for sure, but I'm also beginning to think that Daniel Steele's death wasn't an accident either."

"But it was." Kyle said. "Like I've told you a million times before."

"So let's make it a million and one times shall we? Tell me again, from the beginning, right up to the point when you left your uncle."

"I didn't fuckin' leave him." Kyle protested. "I just went to get him some help."

"Okay, okay." Williams said, raising his hand. "You went to get help. Fine. But let's start from when you first found out that Mehmet was missing and how you knew that something bad was going to happen to him? A *gut feeling* you said?"

Kyle nodded.

"Well. Unless you or any one else convinces me otherwise Kyle." Williams said, with a shrug. "I suggest that's bullshit. So, this is your chance. Convince me."

*

At 9am on Monday 19th June 2017, Kyle was finally allowed to leave the Police station on unconditional bail. OD, Mally and Wing Nut however, hadn't been so convincing and would be remanded in custody for the foreseeable future.

Out in the foyer, Kyle sat down and began to put the laces back into his trainers. They had been removed on request of the custody staff when he was first brought into the station, despite him telling them that he wasn't a suicide risk.

*

"Just policy lad," the custody sergeant had told him. "I've lost count of the number of people that come in here and say they're not suicidal and then try to harm themselves in their cell."

"I'm not that stupid," Kyle had replied.

"No, neither am I Mister Roberts. Laces please?"

*

As Kyle was re-threading his shoes, a door that was opposite to the one he had just come through, suddenly opened and Mehmet stepped out into the foyer. When he saw Kyle sitting there, his initial expression said it all … *awkward.*

"You okay bro?" Kyle asked, concerned.

Mehmet shrugged but didn't reply.

Kyle opened his mouth to speak again - in the hope of breaking the uneasy silence that had followed - but his father Kasim came through the doorway, saw Kyle and shot him a look of disdain.

"Go and wait in the car Mehmet," he said, turning back to his son and handing him the keys.

Mehmet took the keys and turned to walk out of the station. When he got to the main door he stopped and looked back at Kyle. "I'm sorry about your uncle." He offered.

"Thanks mate," Kyle replied. "But it's me that should be apologising to you." Mehmet shrugged again. "I should have done more - could have done more." Kyle quickly added. "But I was … well, I fucked up man." He paused to allow his dry mouth to find what little moisture it could. "I'm so sorry Mehmet, seriously."

"Mehmet. Car!" Kasim directed succinctly, giving his son no chance to carry on the conversation with Kyle and - Allah forbid - re-kindle the friendship between them.

When he'd finally left the building, Kasim turned to Kyle. "You should know that we are leaving Manchester tonight," he said.

"Really?" Kyle replied, surprised. "Where you going?"

"That is none of your concern," Kasim replied, shortly. "I am not telling you about our move

226

because I wish to have a light-hearted chat about it, I am telling you so you understand that this is what you and your delinquent friends have achieved. The disruption of a family who you judged and found guilty merely because they are Muslims."

"Hang about Mister Yilmaz," Kyle interrupted, bitterly. "I never once thought that. I've never judged anybody because of their religion!"

"Be that as it may." Kasim continued. "But I believe that you and your family were - at the very least - complicit in what your uncle had planned, whilst my family might never be the same again. It will take time and patience to repair the damage that has been caused and for this, I know that Mehmet will not forgive you."

"What? But why?" Kyle asked, feeling shocked and hurt by Kasim's words. "Maybe if I speak to him before you go, I can explain that …"

"No," Kasim interjected holding up his hand. "The conversation you have just had with Mehmet was your last. Do you understand? And, if you are as good a friend to Mehmet as you claim to be, then you will respect what I am saying to you and not try to contact him again." Kyle slumped on to the chair and bowed his head. "I pity you Kyle." Kasim continued, causing Kyle to look back up and frown.

"I don't need your pity," he spat, coldly.

"Nevertheless, I do," Kasim went on. "Because as frightened as my family are, as hurt as they might be right now, I still have a family. What exactly do you have?"

Kyle didn't reply nor did he even contemplate challenging Kasim's words. He realised that Kasim was actually right and that hurt more than anything.

"Take care of yourself Kyle." Kasim said and followed his son out of the station.

*

Compared to what the weather had been like previously, the day was unusually warm and sunny especially given that it was only 9am.

Kyle sat on the steps, held his head in his hands and closed his eyes, dwelling once again on what had been and what was yet to come.

The last few weeks had been like an agonising nightmare but this was one he could never wake up from. Maybe, in the unforeseeable future, things would get better but Kyle couldn't see it happening. Not soon, not ever. He was trapped inside it all and it hurt like fuck.

"Cheer up mate, it might never happen!" A chirpy, unfamiliar voice said, immediately snapping Kyle out from his troubled thoughts.

He looked up and stared at the two Police Officers standing in front of him.

"Too late mate," he replied solemnly. "It already has."

The End

Printed in Poland
by Amazon Fulfillment
Poland Sp. z o.o., Wrocław

62308297R00134